Vessel of Miracles

Loredana Rivers

Front Cover Illustration by EJ Frost

Front Cover Design by Loredana Rivers

Back Cover Photograph by Lynn French Photography

Edited by Susan Spicher

US City of Publication: La Vergne, Tennessee

Printed in the United States of America

ISBN: 979-8-218-50372-7

Library of Congress Control Number:
      2024919026

This is my unique gift to the world! I've used the talents that God has blessed me with to craft this story. The purpose of this book is to share my perspective, educate, advocate, entertain, and, most importantly, bring hope to many people!

God uses all His children as vessels in each other's lives to help one another. For example, think about your favorite teacher from when you were growing up. Do you remember the positive influence they had on you? Do you recall how special they made you feel? They served as a vessel in your life, just as you can be for others. Everyone, without exception, has a purpose in this world, including you, dear reader!

This book is dedicated to my Lord and Savior, Jesus Christ! His unwavering guidance and profound love have been a constant inspiration in my life. God's teachings enriched my faith and strengthened me during my most challenging moments. Throughout my journey, I have continually drawn upon His wisdom. It is with deep gratitude that I acknowledge His presence in every step I take.

Mom and Dad, thank you for adopting me and welcoming me into your family as your daughter. Your love and support have been a constant source of strength in my life. I am grateful for your countless sacrifices to ensure my happiness and success over the years. Your belief in my abilities has inspired me to chase my dreams and overcome challenges. It has been a guiding light, illuminating my path even in darker times.
I love you both more than words can convey.
Thank you for everything!

Mrs. Spicher, thank you for all your help with this.
I could not have asked for better! God knew what He was doing when He chose for you to help me with this miracle!

Kelsi, I love you more than all the radiant stars in the night sky! Each twinkle reminds me of the beauty you bring into my life!

Jamie Rhodes's point of view

CHAPTER ONE

Hello! Let me introduce myself. I'm Jamie Metoyer Rhodes, a 43-year-old woman of faith, a single mom, and a successful businesswoman. My life is blessed by my adult son, Richard, who has cerebral palsy. I cherish him more than words can express. I warmly invite you to see what a day in our life is like.

I walked gingerly down the long hallway to my son's room. The clock read 9:00 a.m. It was time to wake Richard up. His nighttime caregiver, Kekoa, just left after sharing care updates and drinking a much-deserved cup of coffee.

If you are wondering why my son has a caregiver, it is because he has a diagnosis of severe cerebral palsy. According to the Oxford

Dictionary, cerebral palsy is defined as
"A medical condition caused by a brain injury or
development problem, usually before or at birth,
that causes the loss of control of movement in
the arms and legs."

Richard was born full-term. However, at the
end of my pregnancy, I experienced severe
abdominal pain and bleeding during the onset of
labor. My uterus had ruptured. That left Richard
without oxygen, resulting in brain damage. The
medical team acted quickly and were able to help
us both. It was the most stressful day of my life
as I prayed desperately for the survival of my
son, who only scored an APGAR of five at one
minute and a risky score of two at five minutes.

Today is Saturday, and I have Richard all to
myself. I quietly opened his bedroom door and
noticed his eyes were open. "Good morning,"
I said as I walked to his bed. Richard must have
just woken up because he did not respond. He
was in his usual sleeping position, on his back
with his legs bent at 45 degrees and rested
toward the right. Richard's eyes appeared heavy
as he stared at the ceiling. Kekoa told me that he
woke up several times throughout the night.

Richard turned his gaze toward me. His eyes
veiled behind a thick layer of curly black hair.

I gently moved his hair out of his face. "Are you cold?" Richard's arms clenched close to his chest. He did that when he was cold. Richard nodded and blinked his affirmative reply.
I grabbed his dark blue blanket and tucked it around him.

"Do you need a little longer to wake up before we get our day started?" Richard slowly nodded. "Would you like to watch a YouTube video while getting motivated to get up?" Richard responded with a nod and a soft guttural hum. Then he looked at me and vocalized a series of short "m" hums. I have always been convinced that he is saying, "Mom." "Do you want me to watch with you?" He smiled his ear-to-ear "yes" grin.

Richard said a deep "Hmmm," followed by his "Mom" sound. "What is it?" I asked. Richard turned his head to the right. Most would interpret this as just a turning of the head. However, I have been interacting with him for 23 years. Despite his inability to communicate by verbalization, we have worked to develop an intricate communication system.

Turning his head to the right means he wants to lie on his right side. Richard is always more comfortable when he is lying down, especially on his side. That allows the spasticity of his muscles to relax. "Okay. Turn as best as you can that way." I positioned myself to assist him in this maneuver. Richard needs a lot of assistance to turn onto his side. "Lean into your right elbow," I said as I placed my right hand behind his left shoulder and my left hand behind his left hip. "Lean into your elbow. There you go." I helped roll him onto his side. Movements like this are difficult for Richard due to spasticity. For a person with cerebral palsy, it can be a life-long struggle. I can't help but think what a miracle it is that he has been able to maneuver as well as he does.

He was so enjoying himself. Richard loves to start his day by watching YouTube on his TV. Many days, watching videos becomes Richard's primary entertainment. He enjoys the sarcasm of his favorite YouTubers. He smiles an open-mouth grin and guffaws with a back-of-the-throat chortle when he "gets it." One of his assistants found an extensive playlist with over 200 videos by his favorite YouTuber! When one video is finished playing, it automatically plays the next one! Genius, if you ask me.

From the beginning of Richard's life, doctors and therapists worked with me to learn the level of care and support he would need. I decided to use our home as the hub for his care. I quickly realized that I needed to surround us with an outstanding team of medical specialists, professionals, and amazing people who would facilitate Richard's daily activities. Richard is my only child. It is just him and I that make up this little family core. However, the caregivers become our extended family.

Richard has a great team of caregivers that rotate throughout the week. Each care provider works an 8-hour shift. Richard needs three people each day to assist him. For each person to be mentally and physically engaged at a high level, I do not have any full-time caregivers. Some only work 16 hours per week.

I have chosen to hire my own providers and not use the services of our state waiver program, which Richard qualifies for as an adult with a disability. I pay well and expect an outstanding level of care for Richard. I'm thankful that, as a business owner, I can afford to give my son excellent home care.

I want to keep quality workers. So, I work to develop a workplace that provides each with job satisfaction. My pay is not the only motivation that creates job satisfaction. I try to make this environment warm, professional, and family-like. Building a relationship with each caregiver is essential to the strategy for Richard's care. That helps develop a happy place to spend the caregiver's time engaged in fulfilling work that makes a difference in this young man's ability to live a productive and fulfilling life.

It is priceless to have top-notch help daily. I cannot do this alone. Looking for caregivers is a hard job. However, it's a more challenging job to find a good one. I'm thankful I've been able to keep this extraordinary team. It can be challenging to afford help willing to work around the clock. I am also aware that many families have trouble getting help in general. Some people have other family members to help them. Others use day programming to accommodate work schedules and give caregivers a break. There are, of course, group homes as your loved one moves into adulthood.

I am a strong advocate for using the resources you have available. They may be personal or be provided through various state and charitable organizations. One should do what fits one's family and circumstances. The goal is to optimize the potential and opportunities for your loved one with exceptionalities. Don't let your financial situation limit what you can provide, as there is always a way to accomplish your goals when you get past the helplessness and move into advocacy. There have been times when I have needed to move into "social justice warrior mode." The result of this tenacity created an improved circumstance for Richard.

I have several qualities and requirements for my hires. I don't want to hire anybody who would treat Richard poorly. I want to make sure we all will be a good match. I don't want to hire someone and then have to let them go. If possible, I would like to get it right the first time. We do not use an agency to hire Richard's caregivers. I personally hire, train, and manage the care providers utilizing the consumer model. Hiring starts with my task of creating a detailed job description delineating what both Richard and I need and expect.

I don't wait for applicants to come to me. Instead, I go out and find them using my network and contacts. I've known one of Richard's caregivers for years. I already trusted her when she said she wanted to work for me. All the other caregivers were suggested to me through my network. As part of the initial vetting process, I take a detailed look at Facebook profiles to get to know the person's character. I am like a detective when I look! I make sure that I like the type of person they appear to be. I will make direct contact if they seem like a good choice.

After that, the potential caregiver and I discussed what kind of assistance Richard needed throughout the day. I also want to know what this applicant wants from this employment relationship. We arrange a neutral meeting place. I am then able to determine how they present themselves professionally as well as personally. How do they speak to me? Are they genuine and polite? Or did they come across as if they only wanted some extra cash? The meeting also allows the potential caregiver to ask me any questions and get a detailed understanding of expectations.

The amount of information gained through the vetting process can be overwhelming. Some caregivers do a great job of deflecting their true agendas. Throughout the entire process, I pray about it and then go with my heart. At this point, we arrange a time for them to meet Richard. I gradually do everything because slow and steady wins the race. I want to see how they interact with him. Would they talk to him like he was a baby? Or would they treat him with respect and dignity? I wanted to see it firsthand. Richard was never afraid to meet anyone, so he wasn't worried about this step.

When the candidate comes to meet us, we tell them a little about ourselves, make them feel at home, and give them a house tour. I demonstrate how I transfer Richard to and from his wheelchair and show them his shower chair. Richard also shares with them using his communication board. He shares about his personal preferences on everything from food to clothing to entertainment. That all allows me to observe the potential for a strong relationship.

Richard and I then discuss the applicant over the next few days. There is no way in this world that I would leave this decision entirely up to me. Richard is the main stakeholder in this situation. He has developed excellent decision-making skills and is able to read people well. He takes time to think about the meeting and then shares his feelings about his ability to work with the person and if they can meet his needs. We discuss both positive and negative attributes. It is a blessing that he is so analytical yet interpersonal. A great example of Richard's care for others is when one rather petite applicant concerned him about transferring. He was unsure if she physically could and did not want her to get injured.

Once Richard and I feel confident about adding to our care team, I call and make the job offer. The training process began with our previous meetings and interactions, but the formal training begins when the job offer is accepted. The way I train his caregivers is extensive, in-depth, and tailored specifically to Richard's needs. One rarely experiences the quality of onboarding that I utilize. I see it as guided on-the-job training! No two days are the same. Some days, Richard could be in the best mood in the world. I say this respectfully, but these days are more manageable. On other days, he might not have slept well the night before or be in pain. That makes him irritable, as it would any of us. These days are more challenging.

I pay close attention to how the caregiver responds to stress and how they physically handle him. Frustration can often be taken out on the client. I thank God that has never happened to Richard. He would let me know if it had. He has learned to speak up.

I will also take the opportunity to share how some of the other care team members or I deal with challenging behavior or situations. Consistency is important for all age levels. Challenging days significantly raise the caregiver's stress level. When mistakes are made, I address the situation to correct it. I know they are learning a lot of new things. The issue is addressed with an opportunity for the caregiver to make adjustments to the procedures. Proper correction should always be done in a way that allows the person to keep their dignity. Just like discipline for a child, it should be a teaching and learning moment for all involved. It is scary to think this person has the potential to take their frustration out on your loved one by mistreating them. People have suggested I put cameras in Richard's room. However, I don't want my home to feel like a supervised prison. I trust the vetting and training process. If necessary, I will release anyone immediately for even a hint of abusive or disrespectful behaviors toward Richard, myself, or anyone else on the caregiving team.

This entire training process is about Richard. Anytime you engage help, it is always about the needs of your loved one. I teach our methods and the processes that are expected to be used in Richard's care. What works for one person will not necessarily work for another.

Richard has unique gestures and ways to communicate his needs. He learned some techniques from various therapists, me, or others he devised on his own. Richard is highly intelligent. His lack of ability to speak, along with spastic movements, causes many to think he has a cognitive challenge.

An example of Richard's physical communication is when he is thirsty; he touches his mouth or swallows hard. To get your attention, he raises his right hand or hums a series of short "m" sounds. That can be like learning a foreign language until one gets to understand Richard better.

A new caregiver would be lost with the way Richard communicates. They must pay close attention to his body language when he is not using his communication board. Plus, they have to learn his cues. That isn't something you master overnight because it takes weeks to train a new caregiver.

During the first week of training, the caregivers only observe. As I assist Richard, they sit back and take notes. They see how I help him when he is having a hard time or giving me a hard time! They observe what I do when he isn't feeling well and how I comfort him. I try my best to do everything in love, just like Jesus would want us to do. Our faith is a fundamental part of who Richard and I are as individuals and as a family. We pay attention to the details of living that enrich us and make us better people.

The second week of onboarding is a little different! The caregivers work hands-on with

Richard while I observe. I am available if a caregiver has trouble or has a question. That allows them to practice what they observed during the previous week. As the week progresses, I will ask them to pretend I am a new caregiver and have them teach me the techniques used for some aspects of Richard's care. Research shows that we retain more than 80% of information that we practice and then teach someone else compared to only 10% retention when we listen to information.

The third week involves me backing off more. I stay around the house and check in periodically. Each day, Richard and I discuss how he feels the process is going. As I see the caregiver and Richard feeling comfortable and confident during the fourth week, I am comfortable leaving the house for short outings. I will extend my excursions as the following week progresses.

I've had the same team of caregivers for quite some time now. I am blessed to have the same people around for so long. It has been lovely getting to know all of them. Caregiving is their passion. They adore Richard and take him seriously. I trust these caregivers so much that I went on a 7-day cruise! That was the first time I went a week without Richard since he was born! My mom lives about an hour away. She packed her bags and stayed at the house with Richard that week. Richard is too grown to admit it, but he missed me! I would FaceTime him a lot while I was gone. He loved that! I was grateful my mom came and stayed while I was on a trip. Richard adores his grandmother! They are very close and always have been. We are blessed to have her in our lives!

During my vacation, I learned an important lesson. When caring for a person with multiple needs, you must also take care of yourself. You think you are okay until you take a time like this. Caregiving can be all-consuming for a family. You need to surround yourself with a reliable and competent support group. It is okay to do things for yourself.

As part of the consumer model that I use in hiring, it is essential that his caregivers feel appreciated and valued. If they feel like they are valued, then they will do a good job. I give them opportunities to get additional education and training that will help them personally and professionally. That leads to more job satisfaction. I like keeping my caregivers the same because they are trained and understand Richard. I consider them to be "the cream of the crop" in terms of the quality of caregivers.

Some days are easier than others. Some days, Richard may not be feeling well. On some nights, he may not sleep at all, no matter how hard he tries to fall asleep. I'm thankful for our team of caregivers. We could not do this without them. Richard needs 24/7 care, and I am grateful for someone who is there to support us through the good and the hard times.

During the day, Richard and his caregiver hang out while I work upstairs. I run a business that I inherited from my dad. If the caregiver needs me, they will send me a text. The caregivers know this is my time to accomplish my own work and provide a comfortable income to keep this family and tribe of caregivers functioning.

I keep my social life healthy by going out with my best friends. Richard calls them his "aunts." I am an only child, so my best friends are like my sisters. All of them adore Richard! They treat him like one of their own and provide me with times of sanity when life gets complicated. They also have children who are around his age. Their children are grown and have moved away for college and career opportunities. Most have moved out of the state and do not visit often. My best friends are empty nesters who now have more time to spend with Richard.

Richard wants to do the same thing as his "cousins." He told me that he wanted a job just like everyone his age. I informed him that I would hire him for my business. I also told him that he needed to think about what he wanted to do. Richard wants to be able to do something on the computer. He has recently started attending classes at our local community college. Richard's caregiver, Sue, attends classes along with him. It has worked out to be a great arrangement!

Sue takes notes for Richard during class as he listens to the lecture. When it is time for Richard to take a test, Sue will take him to the testing center. Richard has extended time on his exams and has his tests read to him. He will then choose A, B, C, or D on his communication board to answer the questions. Recently, Richard has been enjoying the courses on cyber security. He may find this is a career he wants to move into. It would be helpful in my business.

When Richard was younger, I got my Master of Business Administration. My mom was a great help in this accomplishment. I always hoped that, at some point, Richard would have the opportunity to get an education. We all have hopes and dreams for our children. Unfortunately, some think their dreams for a child with exceptionalities can never happen. That is not the case. It just may be different than you imagined.

Richard is also legally blind and has trouble seeing. Because of this, he has two large computer monitors that look more like flat-screen TVs. Richard also has an adaptive keyboard. His large keyboard has big black-and-white keys with letters in extra-large print. Over the years, I have bought him all kinds of adaptive equipment made for computers.

Richard types slowly. He usually hits one key at a time. Along with this, he uses an adaptive computer mouse. His computer mouse does not look like a typical one. It looks more like a stick that is pointing vertically. Richard wraps his hand around it and clicks a button at the top with his thumb. While using the computer, Richard also wears hand splints that help stabilize some of the spastic movements. Even with all of this remarkable technology, his reaction time is slow.

Richard's "Mom" hum roused me from my reminiscent thinking. I looked at him to see what was wrong but knew just by looking. His hair had fallen on his face. I reached over and moved his long back curls away from his eyes. "There you go. I know you love your curly hair, but it sure can cause you some consternation!" I replied, patting his shoulder. Richard chortled with a little affirmative grunt.

Richard has wonderful hair! It is black and curly and reaches right above his shoulders. He will not let me trim the front shorter, so it often falls on his face. I've asked him if it would be okay if I used a bobby pin to keep his hair out of his face. Richard refused because he thinks that's for girls. I explained that it would be used only when he was at home, but that explanation didn't work.

At the moment, Richard was watching a video about school. The YouTuber discussed how neat one of his teachers was. Richard never went to public school because I homeschooled him. I didn't want him to go to school for a multitude of reasons. The main reason is I wanted to be sure he received a quality education that provided him with the tools he needed to be successful in life. The special education system in our area does not really offer individualized education. The fully inclusive model still does not allow the platform to educate a person who lacks verbal skills and has physical limitations. Richard does not have cognitive deficits. He just needs time to accommodate the physical and speech exceptions.

Richard loved being homeschooled.
I knew exactly how he needed to be taught.
I would read things to him and test him just like anyone else. He always got good grades. I often checked with him to see if he wanted to participate in a regular class setting, but he always gave me good reasons why he liked his current schooling arrangement. After he graduated high school, I signed him up for an online college course! I helped Richard with the college course at home. He ended up with an A in that class! I was so proud of him! His success with this course has allowed him to take on-campus courses now.

Growing up, Richard had a few friends. They were my best friend's kids, which we refer to as his "cousins." They were around Richard their entire lives. Richard and I would go swimming at their house. They would also come to our house and watch movies with him. It was delightful! He also made several friends at our church. He enjoyed attending the church's youth group and was often able to go on outings with them. As those friends got older, they graduated high school and just moved on with their lives. When his cousins return to visit their parents, we all get together for dinner and games at our house. Richard is happy to see them, and they entertain us both with stories of their life adventures. That helps Richard get more excited about the possibilities for his own future.

The only people who mainly come to visit Richard besides his caregivers are my mom and his aunts. I have three best friends: Lindsay, Ashley, and Julie. They are like sisters to me. I refer to them as Richard's aunts. They are all very loving and kind to my son. They treat him like an adult and check on him, sometimes daily. Richard loves his aunts very much. We have a giant "family" dinner at our house every Christmas. Richard's aunts always bring him a special Christmas present! Honestly, they spoil him all year round.

Richard was having the time of his life as he laughed at his video. As I said before, he loves sarcasm. He has a great sense of humor, although it sometimes tends to be corny, like "dad jokes." I think he got that from his grandpa. "They are making fun of that poor game. Why are they doing that?" I asked as I laughed along with him and tapped him on his thigh. It is hard to believe that Richard will be 24 next month on September 14th!

"You know your birthday is coming up soon. Do you know what you want?" I asked. Richard shook his head. "Have you thought about it?" He shook his head again. I think I'm more excited about his birthday than he is. I guess I like knowing my son is maturing into adulthood and has a chance to have a party. "How about some new clothes? We can get you plenty of new shirts! Would you like that?" Richard nodded, but I could tell he had something else in mind.

"Consider it done. Would you like to go out to eat on your birthday?" He nodded with a smile. "We can do that too and maybe have a party? Try to think of what else you may want. Think about it for a few days and let me know." Richard nodded as he continued to look at the current video that was playing. I sure wish he was more excited.

I always loved Richard's birthday. It's something he can celebrate. Other people his age are getting married, finishing degrees, or having kids. They are celebrating things like that. I want my son to know that he also has things worth celebrating. He has the same potential to be what his heart desires. His path to his goals just may take a little longer and require more effort and focus.

When Richard turned the big 21, I bought him a new accessible van. Many guys his age decide what vehicle they want to drive, and

Richard is no different. So, he picked out a dark navy blue van with a black interior. Richard has excellent taste! He does not have the dexterity or motor skills required for driving, but the van is still his vehicle. I had to draw the line at putting flames down the sides and one of those obnoxiously loud horns!

Saturday is our day to spend together, and we are not hurried. His caregivers have the day off, and we get to relax. I will take Richard out to lunch because we always have a lunch date on Saturdays. "Hey! Have you thought about where you want to go eat today?" I asked, knowing what the answer would be. Richard smiled his wide-mouth smile in return. "Is it where I think it is? Is it Yamato's?" He nodded. "Okay, noodle head." Richard smiled again. I sometimes call him a noodle head because he always eats Asian-style noodles. It's seriously his favorite food. Plus, Richard thinks this nickname is funny!

Yamato's is where we go 90% of the time. Everyone who works there knows Richard. They are all very kind to him. In the past, when we arrived, they opened the door for us, greeted him with a smile, and moved the chair out of the way at our favorite table. That allows him to be pushed directly up to the table. The waitress there adores him. She will hug him before complimenting his shirt. In return, Richard smiles and points to a word on his communication board. The waitress knows what he wants to order and always makes sure that his drink never gets low! They do not know how much that means to me! I love to see them treat Richard with respect.

Richard started humming. It was not a happy-sounding hum, and it startled me from my thoughts. He did not have a smile on his face. "Is your shoulder hurting?" I asked. Richard nodded. Caregiving often requires some detective work along with trial and error. However, after the number of years I have been caring for Richard, I can anticipate some of his more common patterns. I know Richard has been lying on his right side for a while. His shoulder was starting to feel it.

"Let's get you on your back, sweetie," I said as I gently placed my hand on his left shoulder. Richard can assist me more with turning onto his back from his side. "Do you want to transfer to your wheelchair?" He nodded. I was surprised he did. There are some Saturdays when Richard will stay in bed until noon. After all, Saturday is our relaxing day. During the rest of the week, life can be pretty regimented.

I grabbed the bed remote and elevated the head of the bed. That is how I sit Richard up while he is in bed. It is less strain on his muscles and mine. It is fantastic to have the luxury of this adjustable hospital-type bed. "I know it feels good to change your position. You should ask me sooner when your body needs to be repositioned. You know it is not a bother at all." Richard nodded with a smile and blinked his eyes to say, "Thank You."

I ensured his wheelchair was locked and near the bed. Then, I lowered the bed closer to the floor. Next, I pulled the covers off Richard and placed my right arm around his legs. "Put your arms around my neck." Richard slowly did. After that, I placed my left arm behind his back. In a swooping motion, I brought his legs around to the edge of the bed. Then, I made sure his feet were safely on the ground to ensure a safer transfer.

I hugged Richard and felt a slight squeeze from his arms around my neck. "Are you ready to stand up?" I kept my left arm around his back so he would not fall. He nodded. "On three. Be sure to straighten your legs. You know the drill." I wrapped my other arm around him. "One, two, and three." Richard stood up. Thankfully, he is very strong in his legs when they are stationary. He can stand as long as you are holding him up.

That helps him balance. "Good job. Now, take a step forward." Richard slowly took a step forward as he groaned. "Turn to the right. Take one more step this way," I added as I guided him in front of his wheelchair. "You are there. Please sit down." He did so as I kept my hand on his side.

I grabbed his wheelchair's seat belt and buckled him in. Richard slowly lifted his feet and placed them on the wheelchair's footrest plates. I always let him complete that step because he can do it himself.

Independence in even the smallest and most mundane activities is vital to developing self-esteem. As a parent, I constantly encourage the caregiving team to look for tasks that can be completed independently or with little assistance. I also encourage them to let Richard make decisions. When raising a child, it's important to remember that you are raising a future adult, regardless of their abilities.

CHAPTER TWO

My son has grown up so quickly. It is hard to believe that the baby I held and prayed over has become this competent young man.

From the beginning of Richard's life, he had to fight to overcome so many physical challenges. Even though what seemed like unending hours of stretching and moving his muscles, he always had a smile for his therapists, caregivers, and me. Richard has a combination of hypotonia (low muscle tone), hypertonia (increased muscle tone), and spasticity. Added to the manipulation therapy for these conditions, Richard often used a standing frame. I credit physical and occupational therapy for Richard's remarkable progress in so many areas of his life. That is more evidence that Richard is a vessel waiting to be filled with the miracles of God.

I was encouraged to seek early intervention. My mother, the ultimate researcher, shared endless articles that supported early intervention as a way to "significantly increase the child's ability to learn new skills, overcome challenges, and succeed in life." She has constantly searched for new devices and methods to support Richard and enhance the quality of care and support he has received throughout his life. She was responsible for finding our state-of-the-art ceiling track system to help move Richard throughout our home.

There are tools, devices, and methods appropriate for the variety of tasks and situations that are part of everyday activities for any person. However, Richard requires more strategy to complete what would seem like the simplest tasks. These are often unique to Richard and may change day to day. For example, Richard wanted me to manually transfer him today instead of using his track system. Maybe it was because he was more tired this morning, or he wasn't feeling the effort needed to use the track system.

When transferring Richard, I could tell by his vocalizations that he was in a lot of pain this morning. About 75% of adults with cerebral palsy experience chronic pain. Musculoskeletal pain is very common, but there is an increased probability of migraines, dental problems, and gastrointestinal issues, all of which have other treatment protocols.

Therapy, stretching, exercise, and weight bearing on his legs can ease Richard's pain. That helps him maintain as much muscle strength as possible. The track system has a special harness that can be used to allow him to walk upright. We have also chosen to use baclofen, a muscle relaxer, and warm water therapy. The value of therapy achieved through his daily shower is amazing.

There are also last-resort surgical interventions that can be utilized when other methods have been exhausted. The most common are selective dorsal rhizotomy (SDR), tendon lengthening, tendon transfer, and osteotomy. My prayers and efforts are toward Richard never having to experience these drastic interventions. I firmly believe that the miracles that transpired early in Richard's life will continue to manifest throughout his life.

Richard also takes a daily nap because he has trouble sleeping throughout the night due to his pain. He wakes up two or more times during the night. There are nights when it is every two hours. Last night was one of the every two hours nights.

"So, you woke up a lot last night. Did you have more pain than usual?" I asked while I massaged his knees. Richard grimaced and nodded. "Your knees, again?" Richard hummed. His knees seemed to be the trigger joint for pain throughout his body.

"If you are okay with it, you can shower later tonight. You seem like your pain is better controlled right now. Does that sound good?" Richard nodded and gave me his version of a thumbs-up, which consisted of him raising a clenched fist with his thumb positioned perpendicular to the center knuckle of his index finger. "Hey, my noodle head friend. We better get moving. I am starting to get hungry for our lunch date." Richard smiled. He was easygoing for the most part. I think he was just happy to spend the day with me.

I pushed Richard into his en-suite bathroom. He can also walk to the bathroom or be transported using a full-body lift sling while utilizing his track system. I handed him the hairbrush that was on the counter. Richard smiled as he glanced in the mirror and caught a glimpse of his curly, disheveled mop.

Richard's fingers tightly gripped the brush's handle as he began the battle of the tangled curls. He can only reach the lower part of his medium-length curls. It is difficult for him to hold his arms above shoulder level for more than a few seconds. I took up my front for the battle of the tangled curls from the back and worked my way around. His black curls bounced as I combed through them. "You need to have a trim." Richard shook his head. "You would be surprised what a difference it would make to prevent some of these tangles." I always gave Richard his haircuts at home when he was younger. However, in the last few years, he has wanted the students at the cosmetology school to give him trims.

I stepped back to admire the outcome. "Well, I have to say that you are one handsome young man. I think my hair-styling skills put you over the top!" Richard smiled in the mirror as he evaluated the outcome. Then he hummed what I believe was a "Thank you, Mom." Richard's hair fell onto his face again as he lifted his head to take one more glance in the mirror. "You are very welcome," I replied as I made a scissor-cutting motion and grinned mischievously.

Oral hygiene is essential to the overall health of typically and atypically developing people. One of the earliest skills I helped Richard learn was brushing his teeth. It was not a pretty process, but it was effective. I would sit him on the bathroom counter, wrap a towel around his body, and hand-over-hand brush his teeth while he observed in the mirror. Then, I would spray his mouth with a gentle spray bottle and allow the water and toothpaste to flow into an emesis basin (the little bean-shaped pan used in hospitals) that I held under his chin. This method is easier than trying to move him up to the sink as I had easier access to assist him. Now, there are U-shaped electric toothbrushes that can make things much easier. When Richard was young, electric toothbrushes were not that common, but now that is his preference.

Like many with severe cerebral palsy, Richard has hyperactive drooling. When he is out and about, he carries an absorbent rag that he keeps tucked securely under his leg. There are many things that Richard is capable of physically. Everything is not always easy, but we work with what we have and move on. Richard feeds off of positive energy. That's why I'm always so upbeat. If I weren't, I would be in a chamber of sadness. So, why focus on the things he cannot do? Caregiving is not an easy task. I could wallow in the harsh reality of severe cerebral palsy, but I can't do that. My dad used to talk

about "picking yourself up by your bootstraps."
I did not know what that meant until I watched my
son go beyond what seemed to be humanly
possible to reach a goal. Richard still wears a
smile as he fights his way through. Smiling
seems like his go-to expression for his emotions.

After I helped Richard brush his teeth,
I adjusted the water and applied liquid soap to his
hands. It took several years to get him to the
point where he could effectively wash his hands.
Then, we worked together to apply deodorant
before spraying Richard's favorite Dolce &
Gabbana cologne. "Do you need to go to the
bathroom?" I asked. He shook his head. "Did
Kekoa take you this morning?" He nodded.

Then, Richard awkwardly gripped the
handrims of the wheelchair's wheels and rolled
back toward his room. I bent down to tidy up the
debris left behind from our morning preparation.

After that, I opened his closet and retrieved
two shirts. Like any other adult, Richard wants to
have choices in clothing that represent his
personality. The options were a lovely blue polo
and, his favorite, a dark blue T-shirt with a bowl
of Asian noodles and red chopsticks on the front.
This shirt is an example of Richard's fun side.
"What is your desire for attire today?" Richard

looked at me before his head turned towards the noodle shirt. "You always wear that shirt every time you go." Richard chuckled and grinned.

Richard's shirts were always a size larger because it made it easy to get his arms in and out. The spasticity in his arms and shoulders makes getting a pullover shirt on more difficult. However, this type of shirt is often more comfortable to wear when transferring and moving about in a wheelchair. I removed Richard's current T-shirt before I placed the neck over his head from front to back, stretching it slightly. Richard moved his clenched fist toward the right armhole, and I assisted him with pushing his arm through by gently pushing upward on his bent elbow. We repeated this motion for his left arm, which was extra tight today. Richard grimaced slightly and I decided to lighten the mood a little. "People are going to think this is your only shirt!" Richard laughed his wide-mouth laugh! I know that I sometimes embarrass him, but isn't that a mom's job?

We moved on to dressing the lower half of Richard's body. After 23 years, we have developed techniques to expedite this process. Most importantly, we have created a process that all his caregivers can duplicate. Consistency is an important tool in the caregiver's tool chest.

When caring for a person with an exceptionality, like cerebral palsy at Richard's level, it is important to remember that the caregiver's body must also be protected. Learning and practicing proper lifting, transfers, and movements can reduce injuries to the caregiver and the person being cared for.

I rolled Richard next to his royal blue electric wheelchair. Then I grabbed a pair of black jeans and bunched them up. I ensured the top and bottom of the pants legs were close together. I took Richard's right leg and slid it into the right leg hole. I did the same for his left leg before I brought the pants up as high as possible on his legs. That way, they would be easier to grab when I pulled them up.

After that, I put on Richard's socks and shoes. "Your feet are flat on the floor. Here we go." I locked his manual wheelchair and placed my arms around his back. Richard slowly leaned forward as he pushed with his legs. I'm grateful that he is strong enough to stand up. "We are almost done." I pulled his pants up and buttoned them.

Then, I pivoted Richard's body into his electric wheelchair. "You are all ready for the day!" Richard placed his feet on the footrests as

I buckled the seat belt and adjusted his leg rests to support his calves. Then, I grabbed Richard's wheelchair tray. The tray attaches by placing it over the wheelchair's armrests. It also holds his laminated communication board. I slid the tray into the locks that keep it firmly in place. Richard rested his arms over many squares that contained words and colorful pictures.

Richard reached out in an attempt to take my hand as he verbalized his "Mom" hum to get my attention. I took his left hand. He moved his right hand and touched the word "go" on his communication board. "Are you ready to go?" He smiled and nodded. I guess patience was not a virtue he was displaying this morning. "I'm not ready to leave yet. I still have to finish getting ready," I said before I turned on his electric wheelchair. Richard sighed. "It will take only a few minutes." Richard slowly maneuvered his electric wheelchair forward as I turned off the TV and lights in his room.

As Richard waited in the hallway, I walked into my walk-in closet. I quickly changed outfits and brushed my hair. I knew I wouldn't have time to do my makeup completely today. Luckily, I did the basics this morning before Kekoa left. Saturdays don't give me much "me" time, but I am okay with that. I have been able to develop several shortcuts for the process of getting myself ready for the day. Caregivers must learn to use every moment of the day to their advantage. You never know when there may be an unavoidable glitch in the day.

"Richard, are you ready? Oh! I almost forgot! I didn't put on any perfume. I want to smell as wonderful as you do," I called out as Richard laughed from the hallway.

I walked down the hallway and opened the door to the garage. Richard gradually passed through the doorway. We then went down the ramp into the garage, where Richard's blue chariot awaited. Richard motioned toward my hand, which held the keys. "Yes, you can go ahead and let down the ramp." I placed the keys on Richard's tray.

There is a push button that slides the door open, lowers the van, and then extends and lowers the side entrance ramp. No matter how often I see this happen, I still think it is the coolest thing ever! I placed Richard's thumb over the button. As I steadied his thumb on the button, he pressed his thumb down.

Richard slowly maneuvered his electric wheelchair up the ramp. He practiced for almost five years to be able to do that. The van has ample space where the passenger seat would usually be. That is where Richard parks his wheelchair. Richard gradually rolled into place before he made minor adjustments. We placed reflective tape on the passenger door to help him know when to stop moving forward so he could better align himself. I secured his wheelchair to the van's floor using the adjustable tie-downs. I tugged at the tie-downs to ensure they were tight. I then pressed the ramp's button and got into the driver's seat. "We are finally on our way!" Richard grinned big! He was so excited to be getting out and about! I turned up the radio. He never seemed to care about what we listened to.

Richard always seems content when we are driving around. He loves to watch the world as it goes by. On longer road trips, Richard often lets out a loud hum when he sees some of his favorite buildings. He loves the tall city skyscrapers the most. However, his favorite time to drive around is Christmas. He admires all the Christmas light displays.

Before we knew it, I pulled into Yamato's parking lot. I call this "Richard's second home." He loves the food and the people here. I parked in an accessible parking space before we started the disembarking process.

If we were going to eat at any other restaurant, we would google and review the menu beforehand. I would read the entire menu to Richard. We would figure out what he wanted before we went inside. If I read a food item that he liked, Richard would nod his head. Finding out what he wants to eat can take a long time. So, doing that beforehand makes ordering food a breeze.

"Before we get inside, you should think about what you want to eat." Richard smiled as I motioned for him to back up and turn his wheelchair to go down the ramp. "I will take that as you want your favorite order of noodles."

I anticipated a delightful meal and some time with the wonderful staff here.

CHAPTER THREE

Richard's smile broadened as he eased his way
down the van's ramp. He then glanced over his
left shoulder back toward the van. Before I forgot,
I grabbed my Louis Vuitton purse. "Yes, son.
I have the keys and my purse. I am closing the
ramp and locking the van." Richard knows I can
get distracted and feels he must look after me.
I have to admit it is nice to have an extra brain.

Richard continued toward the restaurant's
entrance. A gentleman kindly opened the door.
"I appreciate it!" I beamed with a grateful smile.
Richard smiled and nodded. "You are welcome.
You two have a good day." Richard grinned.
I love it when people are friendly and show
compassion by offering common courtesy!

"Hello, Richard!" a cheerful voice greeted him. It was Richard's favorite waitress, Lin. "How are you? Are you doing well?" she asked. Richard nodded. Was that a slight blush I saw on his cheeks? I noticed that he had an extra special twinkle in his eyes. Lin gently patted his arm. "I have a table ready over here, Ms. Rhodes."

The manager, Mr. Kajiyashiki, obviously saw us pull into the parking space and had already requested his staff to prepare a table for us. Besides the food at Yamato's, we love the entire staff. They live up to the meaning of their name. The Yamato Dynasty in Japan was one of the largest and most well-known from 210 to 710 AD. The term Yamato has become known to represent the Japanese persona of greatness and harmony.

We followed Lin to a nearby table with a pleasant fountain view. Richard rolled himself right beside the table. "I like your shirt, Richard." "He always wants to wear this shirt when he comes here. I promise he has other shirts." Richard gave Lin his best thumbs up and said, "Aahh uh." "Richard said thank you." Lin smiled. "You are very welcome!"

"What can I get you to drink?" Lin asked as she flipped the menu over and placed it before

Richard. "Do you want a coke?" I asked. Richard nodded and tapped on the Coke emblem that was on the back of the menu. He then gave Lin a sideways glance and grin. "I will have water." "Sounds good. Would you like me to put that in a cup with a lid?" "Yes. Can you please put our drinks into to-go cups with lids?" "Sure. I will have those for you shortly." I always ordered Richard's drinks in a to-go cup with a lid. That prevents a spill if he accidentally knocks it over. I don't want him to feel singled out, so I also get my drink in a to-go cup with a lid. I want Richard to know that we are in this together.

I placed my arm around Richard's shoulder. He was watching a nearby flashing sign that was changing colors. He loved anything that lit up and looked incredible! I patted his shoulder as we waited for our drinks. Richard was smiling the entire time, and I wondered what he was thinking.

Even with his communication board available, Richard had little to say. I don't know if that is his true personality. Maybe he is used to only thinking his thoughts, so he naturally keeps them inside. What if it may be too much work for him to tap out every thought he has? There are still so many things that I do not know about Richard. That's why I always encourage him to tell me what he thinks. I try to help him break that barrier of silence when he can.

Richard can also spell out words on his communication board. He does this when he has something to say that is not a word choice. He has the alphabet and the numbers 0 to 9 on his communication board. Sometimes, Richard spells out words, but it takes him a very long time.

It's important to slow down and be attentive when communicating with Richard. It takes him longer to engage in conversations, but the effort is worthwhile. It takes him five times longer to respond. For instance, if you ask a simple question, it may take at least three minutes for him to spell out an answer. While this may initially feel awkward, you become used to it with time.

Another thing is that I never know what Richard is thinking behind his eyes. Let me give you a better idea of what this is like. Let's say that you are standing beside someone at the store. Do you know what they are thinking? Of course, you don't. You can't read their thoughts. Then that person tells you that you look nice! You had no way of knowing that they thought that about you. The only way you found out was because they told you.

Now imagine having a son who can't let you know his thoughts. He keeps them to himself

75% of the time and struggles to tell you the other 25%. It can be very challenging. That's why I treasure every little thing and detail that Richard tells me. His thoughts are priceless to me.

I spotted a child in the booth beside us. He was looking at Richard. I was used to people doing that by now. I understand they are curious, and that is okay. It's not every day that you see a guy using a wheelchair and a communication board or using a variety of sounds to talk. Well, it is every day for me!

I don't know how often Richard notices when people stare at him. I remember one time when Richard noticed. I told him they were looking at him because they thought he was cute. I want to protect my son, but it is also important to help him learn how to respond to people who don't know about him. So, I take the opportunity to help people meet and begin to understand and appreciate Richard. We have noticed that some people think Richard has cognitive challenges because he does not immediately respond to questions. The reality is most people with cerebral palsy have normal intellectual abilities. Richard and I teach people we meet about the exceptionalities that he overcomes.

I smiled at the child. "Hi, sweetie. How are you today? I see that you have been looking at my son. Would you like to meet him?" "I am so very sorry!" the child's mom exclaimed. "No worries. It is okay. Richard, would you like to meet this little boy who thinks your wheelchair is super cool?" Richard wrapped his fingers around the joystick, backed his wheelchair up, and swung around to the booth where the child stood on the seat. "This is Richard. What is your name?" "Sammy," he replied shyly. Richard reached out his hand and lightly touched hands with little Sammy. "Sammy, I saw you were watching Richard. He uses a wheelchair to help him move around because his muscles don't let his body do all the things your body can do. However, Richard loves to meet new people." Richard grinned and nodded. "I like your chair wheels," Sammy said as he touched Richard's electric wheelchair.

"Sammy, if it is okay with your parents, you be sure to come and say goodbye to Richard before you leave." Sammy nodded and smiled. "Bye, Richard." Richard gave Sammy a little wave. He then turned his wheelchair around and rolled beside the table just as our drinks arrived.

I smiled and winked at Richard. "I am so proud of how you responded to Sammy." Richard smiled back. For a brief moment, I thought about what it would be like to have grandchildren. I love young children and their energy levels, constant chatter, and unique ways of expressing their thoughts. Could I dare hope that, at some point, Richard would be able to have his own family?

"Here are your drinks," Lin said as she handed both drinks to me. "Thank you." I sat Richard's drink down in the middle of his tray. Richard could reach his straw if I placed his drink in the middle. Lin bent beside Richard and asked, "What would you like to order?" Richard put his right knuckle over the "7" on his communication board. "I'll have the number four." I try to get something different every time I come. On the other hand, Richard always gets the same thing. "I will take your orders to the back. Do you need anything before I leave?" Richard shook his head. "Okay. I will be back soon."

Richard struggled to sip his drink. On the inside, I felt terrible for him. I hated how everything had to be a challenge for him. Richard often has a hard time controlling his arms and hands. It is like he has to will them to do what he wants. Richard's elbows and wrists are always bent, his fingers clench tight, and his thumbs are usually between his middle and index fingers.

I held his cup to keep it steady. He took a drink. "I am sorry that I forgot to bring some Dycem. I knew there was something I was forgetting."

Throughout Richard's life, my mom and I searched for tools to help him accomplish everyday living tasks. One occupational therapist suggested we invest in Dycem, a non-slip material that can be cut into different sizes. This rubberized material stabilizes items so they do not slide around.

Richard made eye contact with another person seated at a table across from us. The young man smiled at Richard and nodded a greeting. Richard smiled back and nodded in return. Richard loves to watch people and see how they act in various situations. I just wish there were more ways for him to communicate.

Richard has utilized various forms of communication boards since he was a child. His difficulty with fine motor skills made it hard for him to communicate quickly. I remember him getting frustrated as he tapped out detailed responses. When Richard was younger, I used a picture exchange communication system called PECS. It was fairly easy for Richard to point at the pictures. He learned to put together sentences and read using PECS. We even added some of our own pictures using photos of various family members, friends, and places.

It is difficult to build relationships if a person cannot verbally interact with others. As Richard progressed through his home-schooling curriculum, I tried to be sure he was learning to express himself so he could connect with others. We had plenty of interactions with other families who chose to home-school. Richard would "chat" with other children his age, but it took a while for him to warm up to them.

In the past, Richard attended speech therapy. He was always eager to go. As Richard got older, his speech therapist educated me on AAC. AAC stands for augmentative and alternative communication. His speech therapist said, "Augmentative and alternative communication offers crucial methods to support or replace spoken and written language for those with communication challenges."

Richard's speech therapist wanted him to use an iPad to communicate. The iPad is a form of AAC. The iPad has special software installed that displays many categories and words. You can tap the screen to change which words are available. For example, say you wanted to tell me what you wanted to eat. All you would need to do is hit the "food" icon. Then, the screen would change and display many food items in little boxes. The food item's name would be at the top of the box, while a small picture would be underneath.

In an instant, I would have gladly paid for that communication software! However, Richard needs his words and letters to be in a large, bold font. We decided to give this method a try. In therapy, they laid an iPad on Richard's tray. The communication software would be ready for him to use. Unfortunately, Richard could not see the words and letters on the iPad. He also would touch words and letters that he didn't mean to. For instance, his hand would jerk, causing him to select a word unintentionally. The therapist tried putting a keyguard on the iPad. That was to help prevent Richard from touching the wrong word. Even with the keyguard, Richard could not point his finger and tap the screen. He had trouble placing his finger inside the keyguard to select the word he wanted.

Even though that method didn't work, we had to try again. I believe if one option doesn't work, try another. I cannot stress that enough. Never give up. Everyone has a voice and deserves to be heard.

After that, we installed a different speech application. We hoped the words would be larger and more accessible. Sadly, there was not much of a difference. Luckily, Richard's speech therapist told me about a Tobii Dynavox eyegaze communication device. Richard would not have to use his hands to operate it. I was always willing to learn about new methods to try. The speech therapist explained that the device tracked the movement of your eyes. You can look at a screen and select a word or letter with your eyes! I thought that was beyond fascinating! I had no idea that something like that even existed! Props to all the people who collaborated to invent this!

Fortunately for Richard, the speech therapist had one at the clinic to try out! The communication device looked like a black screen. At first glance, I thought it was a small TV! Richard found that hilarious! The therapist placed the device on a silver mount. She instructed Richard to look ahead at the screen. Richard listened to his therapist. He was always so polite to them. I was very thankful that he didn't give them a hard time. I always counted my blessings on this journey.

When Richard looked ahead, a small cursor appeared on the screen. It showed where his eyes were looking. On the screen, there were words and pictures inside colorful boxes. The therapist explained that she chose the word size based on the number of words displayed on the screen. She only displayed ten words and intended to make them as large as possible. On a side note, you may have wondered why Richard doesn't wear glasses. The eye doctor said that glasses wouldn't improve Richard's eyesight. I never understood why, but I'm not an optometrist.

Then, the therapist asked Richard to look ahead and select the word "want." His therapist even pointed to the word to show him where to look. Richard looked ahead. The cursor moved all over the screen. It took him some time to land on the correct word. After Richard found the right word, he focused his eyes on it. In no time, the word "want" was spoken aloud from the device.

This continued for a while. The therapist pointed to a word that she wanted Richard to select. After that, he would attempt to choose that word with his eyes.

Unfortunately, Richard could not accurately select the words on the device's screen. The device's camera could not capture Richard's eyes to create functional use. His eyes and the device did not get along. I asked Richard if he could easily read the words. He shook his head. I noticed that the picture in each box was larger than the word. That gave me an idea! I knew there was a way for the speech therapist to fill the boxes with pictures instead of words. I thought Richard could see the "hands reaching for a red box" icon and remember that it means the word "want." So, I asked Richard if he could remember each word based on the picture in the box. Richard appeared stressed as he shook his head. The thought of remembering what word each picture stood for had to be overwhelming to him.

Sometimes, my brain wants to grasp onto hope so badly that I think unrealistically. I will tell you firsthand that I still struggle with this today. I will do anything for Richard because I want the best for him.

Overall, it was a remarkable experience. I am very grateful that a piece of technology like the Tobii Dynavox exists! It can help a lot of other people.

In conclusion, Richard prefers a communication board. It is ironic to me because he loves all things technology. However, this situation is different. He appreciates the visibility of the bold letters and words. He also likes that he won't make a mistake if his hand slips. If that happens, he only needs to move his hand and try again. Richard can also see better if the words are projected on a giant computer monitor. On the computer, he can zoom in to enlarge things. That makes all the difference in the world to him. Richard can do much more on the computer. He can type in what he wants to search for and everything! It's remarkable!

Regarding communicating with Richard, I had to learn to accept things for what they are. I used to try so hard to have Richard talk to us in the way that we considered normal. Rather, it is made possible through communication devices, communication boards, etc. Even though he has a communication board, Richard doesn't use it as much as I hoped. I have to meet him where he is. I have learned to adapt my language to his. That means I must be okay with him communicating through body language, humming, and smiling.

I want Richard to be happy. I am okay as long as he is happy. Many times, I have asked him if he was alright. He would nod with a smile. That helps my heart a lot. However, the most important thing that I realized is that love wins in the end. That means that I know without a doubt that we love each other. When you have love, you have a solid foundation to get through anything. Even when I can't "hear" Richard, love wins. Even on his most silent days, love wins. Even when his thoughts are unreachable, love wins. In the end, love will always prevail in any challenging situation. That's because I know it's there. There is nothing too hard that Richard and I will face that will take away the love between us.

Richard hummed out his "Mom" hum. "What is it, sweetie?" He motioned toward the fountain. The fountain alternated between various water and light patterns. "That looks incredible. I saw an amazing fountain display at the Bellagio in Las Vegas. They have it timed with different music."

To my surprise, Lin was already back with Richard's food. His order was simple. He liked the udon noodles with Sriracha sauce. "It's hot and fresh," Lin informed Richard as she handed his plate to me. She was unsure where to place it since Richard's cup was on his wheelchair's tray. "Thank you very much! We appreciate it." Richard grinned.

I moved Richard's drink to his left side and put the plate of noodles on the center of his tray.

Then I took his hand and prayed, "Dear God, thank You for today. Thank You for the time that Richard and I can spend together. Lastly, thank You for our wonderful food. Amen." Richard smiled in agreement.

I tucked a napkin in the front of Richard's shirt before I twisted some noodles tightly onto the fork and held it close to his mouth. Richard leaned forward and took a bite. "Hey, Richard, your momma has to feed you your food?" Sammy had walked over to say goodbye as his family prepared to leave. His mom came behind him and tried to cover up her embarrassment. "You never know what kids will say! I am sorry Sammy is bothering you."

"Sammy is not a bother. He is just curious about what he is seeing. Yes, I feed Richard because his hands have a hard time using a fork." Richard looked at Sammy and agreed with a nod. "Uh oh! Your momma missed your mouth. You have food on your face." Sammy grabbed a napkin and wiped Richard's chin. My heart melted because he helped Richard.

Sammy patted Richard's arm. "I have to go now. We are going to buy some new shoes. My old shoes are too small." Richard smiled and hummed a goodbye. Sammy then skipped off behind his parents. "He is such a sweet little boy." Richard nodded and opened his mouth as I brought up another fork of noodles.

I appreciated how Sammy was kind to Richard. Not everyone is like that. Richard and I have encountered some pretty rude people. I never can understand why people assume Richard doesn't have normal feelings or understand what they are saying. People sometimes talk to him like he is a baby or talk extra loud as if he has trouble hearing.

There was a time when someone I knew for years thought Richard could not understand anyone. He does! When in doubt, just ask. If you need clarification, ask him if he understands! He will nod his head! A friend once told me, "Jamie, his intelligence is trapped inside." Richard's intelligence is not trapped. People need to listen to him. If they listen, then they will hear him. People need to give Richard the same courtesy as anyone else and get to know him for his unique ways of maneuvering through life.

"That looks delicious," I said as Lin placed my food on the table. Then she reached over and sat a pair of chopsticks by Richard's plate. "I thought you might like these so you get the full udon noodle experience." Richard laughed!

"That's so thoughtful! Thank you!"

"Do you need a refill?" Lin asked. "Not at the moment. Can I get an extra plate, please?" I requested before I took a bite of my food. "I will get that for you." Richard smiled as he moved his left arm closer to the chopsticks. "Go ahead and see if you can work them. I learned the trick of teaching people how to use chopsticks. I just saw it on a video. You need a rolled-up piece of paper and a rubber band. Would you like me to show you?" Richard nodded. "Let's see. I have a ponytail holder in my purse. I will also use one of my deposit slips from my checkbook to roll up for the paper." I rolled the paper up and made about a half-inch cylinder. I placed it two inches from the bottom between the chopsticks and then wrapped the ponytail holder around. That created a fulcrum that worked like a pair of tongs. "Here is how it works." I demonstrated the basic use and placed it in Richard's hand. He laughed at himself as he tried to squeeze the upper end together to pick up a noodle. He finally managed to pinch one. It only took five or six attempts. Richard looked pleased with himself.

Lin handed me a beautiful cream-colored plate. "Thank you!" "You are very welcome." I placed some of my food on the plate. Richard often wanted to sample a little of my food.

I prepared his fork with some rice and fed it to him.

I started to think about how thankful I am that Richard can swallow with no trouble. Swallowing is a common challenge for people with cerebral palsy. That usually is because of dysphagia or oral-motor dysfunctions. Difficulties with swallowing can lead to problems with respiratory health and hinder proper nutrition.

Richard raised his hand and hummed. "What's up?" He yawned and lifted his hand to cover the yawn. I wiped his chin.

Fatigue and extreme exhaustion are common among individuals with cerebral palsy. Research indicates that up to 40% of adults with cerebral palsy experience greater levels of fatigue compared to the general population. For a person with cerebral palsy, moving around can require up to five times more energy than it does for someone without the condition.

A teenage girl approached our table and said, "Hey, man! I love your shirt!" Richard smiled. I instantly knew why. The girl sported a shirt similar to his! She wore a red Japanese-style shirt with various foods on it. Noodles were one of them! "My name is Lexus. What's yours?" she asked. "Allow him to tell her himself," I told myself as I moved his plate away from his communication board.

Richard looked down at his communication board and focused on all the letters. With his visual challenges, he has to look closely at the letters and words. Richard slowly placed his right knuckle on the "R." Lexus bent beside him and patiently looked at the communication board. Then Richard moved his right knuckle to the letter "I." He continued to do this slowly as he tapped "C," "H," "A," "R," and finally "D." "I love your shirt, Richard. Mine is similar. When I saw yours, I got so excited! You have a good style in clothing!" Richard smiled and gently moved his hand to the square that read "Thank you." "You are welcome!" Richard then pointed at her shirt. "Do you like mine too?" He grinned! "What did you order?" Richard gestured toward his plate of noodles. "Nice! I usually get the stir-fry plate! Maybe I will try those sometime. What are they called?" Richard placed his right knuckle over the "7" on his communication board. "The number seven! I'll have to try that next time! Who is this with you?" Lexus asked. "I am his mom," I said proudly.

I loved watching Lexus and Richard have that conversation. There was no communication barrier between them because she took the time to be caring and polite. Many people do not try to be friendly toward Richard. Lexus did, and I knew that made Richard happy. I noticed he had confidence in himself when he smiled during that conversation. I wished everyone could see Richard through God's eyes and know his value.

"It was nice to meet both of you! I just had to come and look at your awesome shirt." Richard attempted to wave goodbye. "Have a great rest of your day, Lexus." Richard grinned as Lexus walked away.

"Are you excited?" Richard flashed a smile! I wish I knew what he was thinking. People say a smile says a million words. It does. However, I would love to know Richard's million words. Maybe he was thinking, "Wow! That girl is so nice! I enjoyed our conversation!" Or perhaps he was thinking, "I like her shirt. Where did she get it? I would like to have one like that." Who knows?

Richard rubbed his right eye and yawned again. "Are you ready to go home?" To my surprise, he shook his head. "No!" I exclaimed. Richard nodded.

Lin walked to our table and said, "Here are your to-go boxes and check." "Thank you! I hope you have a good rest of your day." "You do the same. Bye, Richard! See you next time," Lin said as she wrapped her arm around him. Richard leaned his head into her arm. That moment would have made a great picture!

I put my leftovers inside a to-go box and did the same for Richard's. Then, I set the boxes on his tray. "Please hold these for me." I placed cash on the table with a generous tip because Lin deserved every penny.

I removed the napkin from Richard's shirt. "Ready to roll?" He laughed. I always tried to make things fun for him. "As soon as we get situated in the van, you will need to tell me what you want to do." Richard nodded and rolled toward the entrance. "Please be sure to come back soon. We always enjoy serving you," Mr. Kajiyashiki said as Richard grinned and nodded enthusiastically. I knew he would make sure we lived up to that promise.

I opened the door for Richard, and he rolled outside with no trouble. "You have your hands full. I will lower the ramp." He grinned as he placed his arm around the to-go boxes. He loved to help when he could.

The van's ramp lowered. I took the to-go boxes and chopsticks before Richard carefully rolled up the ramp. As he adjusted his wheelchair in place, I put everything on the van's back-row seat. Then, I secured his wheelchair with the tie-downs. "Ready to go, Mr. Rhodes?" Richard laughed. He enjoyed being called that nickname!

"Tell me where you want to go. Please spell out the name of the place." Sometimes, Richard would spell "store," and I never knew which one. Then, I would have to ask him to spell the store's name. To save him some time, I told him to spell the place's name. Richard bowed his head as he fixed his eyes on his communication board. The letters and words have been in the same location for years.

"What letter does the place start with?" I asked in an attempt to break the task down for him. Sometimes, I try to guess what Richard is trying to spell. That doesn't always work out. It distracts him and makes him lose his place. Richard gently moved his index finger over the letter "M." "Macy's?" I guessed. Richard nodded. "We have a winner!" It is funny that my adult son wants to go to Macy's!

Then, I thought of an idea! "Do you want to see if Aunt Ashley wants to come too?" Richard happily vocalized. I retrieved my phone and called her.

"Hey, Jamie!" Ashley answered. "What are you doing? Richard wants to know if you will come shop at Macy's with him." Richard threw his head back and laughed. "Are you sure you don't want to go, Jamie?" "Richard wants you to come! I think you need to join in on the experience." "I wouldn't miss it! The good news is that I am already in town. I will meet you there. Be sure to tell Richard that I love him." "Okay. We will see you soon."

I hung up and said, "Richard, your aunt can come. She also wanted me to tell you that she loves you." Richard pointed at the steering wheel. He was ready to go!

CHAPTER FOUR

I knew the drive to Macy's would be short. Richard smiled as I turned on some music. He didn't seem as tired as before because he was perking up.

As I drove through town, we passed many tall, beautiful buildings. Richard looked out the window, lost in thoughts I would never know. Some days, it seemed as if Richard's thoughts were so far away and out of reach.

As bad as this may sound, I wonder if I even know Richard. Yes, I know him, but do I truly know him as the man he is? That is a dilemma for every parent as their child matures into adulthood. However, I think it is intensified for me because everyday conversations with Richard are challenging. What I know about him is very limited. It breaks my heart because I want to know him so much more.

People have told me that I am Richard's voice. I respectfully disagree. I am not Richard's voice. I am his advocate. He is his own individual. Richard deserves autonomous communication! Would you want someone else to talk on your behalf? That person would sometimes correctly guess what you think. In reality, they would guess wrong the majority of the time.

Guessing Richard's thoughts is not always the best route. I don't want to put words in his mouth. Most of the time, my guesses are wrong if it's for something complicated. How would you feel if someone said you thought a certain way about something? How would you feel if someone incorrectly guessed your thoughts before saying them aloud?

Sometimes, I'm forced to guess Richard's thoughts. I hate doing that because this process can be a mess. I know that guessing is sometimes necessary. It can be quicker than Richard spelling out the issue letter by letter. Realistically, that can take him a very long time. All of this is a process. It takes time to learn and master his recurring patterns. For example, if something is wrong, it is usually because Richard is in pain or wants to turn onto his side. It took me years to learn Richard's "thought process." Sometimes, my guesses are very far off. There are times when I think his back is hurting, and it ends up being that he wants to look something up online.

I strive to give Richard the tools he needs to enrich his life and mature into the person he is meant to be. I love Richard's personality and character. He is loving, kind, and cares deeply about people. You can see how his heart breaks when he sees a homeless person on the side of the road. Several times, he has asked me to stop and give the person one of our to-go boxes.

People may shy away from Richard because they don't understand him. However, I will work endlessly to advocate for him and others who need to be understood.

"I love you." Richard looked at me and smiled. I loved it when he smiled. He did not know how much his smile meant to me. Richard's smiles served as a source of encouragement to help me keep going. If he can be content, then so can I.

Then Richard pointed to a place on his communication board. I cannot see which word he points to while I'm driving. In this situation, he responds a lot by humming. Each of Richard's hums has a personality of its own. He has complete control over making that vocal sound. His hums can be soft and sweet, while others are forceful with an attitude. Some hums even have a question mark at the end, similar to how we hum when we question something. That's how I know if he is asking or wondering something! I'm thankful that Richard can control the tone of his hums. They point me in the right direction to better understand his thoughts.

"I'm sorry, but I can't see what that says. You can tell me when the van is parked. We are close to being there! I can see Macy's from here." Richard wasn't bothered at all.

I pulled into a large parking lot. It was less busy than I expected. I drove towards the front of the store and parked in a van-accessible parking space. I was thankful nobody parked in the space marked with diagonal lines. People think these are for "run in and run out" parking. These lines reserve space for the wheelchair ramp to lower, providing enough room for a wheelchair user to exit the vehicle. Unfortunately, some people abuse the use of these parking spaces. Basic human kindness should allow a little grace for those who need this minor accommodation.

There was a time when someone else parked over the diagonal lines. Richard and I were coming back to the van after shopping. Because someone parked over those diagonal lines, we had nowhere to let down the ramp. I didn't know whose vehicle it was, and the driver was nowhere in sight. I had no option but to back up the van into the parking lot's travel lane. People were looking at us, but it was not our fault. There was no other way for Richard to get into the van.

"No one parked over the lines today. Let's hope nobody parks there while we are gone." Richard smiled as I pressed the button that lowered the ramp. A buzzing sound filled the van. The right side door slid open before the van lowered like an elevator! Then, the ramp slid out. It was a noisy process that took us forever to get used to!

I exited the driver's seat, walked behind Richard, and released the retractable tie-downs. As Richard carefully rolled down the ramp, I made sure his wallet was in my purse.

Richard likes to make his own purchases. He has a credit card that we use to develop solid budgeting skills. He does pretty well. The rule is if you can't pay off your credit card bill at the end of each month, it goes away, and you must make every purchase using cash. Richard prefers to use a credit card. It only took one time of card quarantine to be convinced of that!

As we approached the entrance, I saw Ashley wave. She was already coming toward the entrance. I waved back and smiled. "Richard, Aunt Ashley is already here." Richard grinned big.

Macy's has automatic doors at the entrance. We usually go to places that we know are accessible. There were times when Richard could not go inside a store or restaurant, and we had to change our plans.

There are plenty of ways for a building not to be accessible. For example, the entrance could have multiple doors. It is a challenge if you have nobody to help open them. Sometimes, an accessible door switch is available, but it may not be functioning. Fortunately, I help Richard open the door. These situations make me think about other wheelchair users who may not have help.

Restrooms and store aisles are another issue. Even though the Americans with Disabilities Act requires accessibility for public buildings, everyone's definition of accessibility is different and poorly executed.

Whenever I want to take Richard somewhere new, I research the location ahead of time. I used to call and ask if the place was wheelchair accessible. Sadly, everyone's idea of "accessible" is not the same. Sometimes, the entrance would have several steps, or an area would be too narrow. Well, I don't call ahead of time anymore. Instead, I look at photos of the place beforehand. I see if there are any steps at the entrance because not all locations have ramps. Thankfully, Richard's favorite stores and restaurants are accessible! That is a significant win in my book!

We entered the store and noticed it was busier than usual. I was surprised because the parking lot was not that full. Ashley hugged Richard. "Hello, my lovely bonus kid! How are you?" Richard smiled as he listened to her. Ashley is a little energetic and always provides free entertainment for Richard! He enjoys her company and thinks she is hilarious!

I hugged Ashley. I was always delighted to see her. "Come on, man! Let's go spend your hard-earned money. What are we shopping for today?" Richard grabbed the corner of his collar and grinned at Ashley. I laughed and said, "Do not forget that he wears a size larger than his actual size. I usually look for a medium."

Ashley and I followed Richard down the aisle toward men's wear. He then raised his hand. "What is it?" Richard pointed toward a dark teal-blue shirt. "Richard! Get out of here! You are expanding your wardrobe colors!" Ashley exclaimed as she quickly flipped through the shirts to find a medium. Richard nodded. "They have a medium!" Ashley placed the shirt on Richard's chest and laid a sleeve across his arm so he could see it better.

Ashley motioned for Richard to come to a nearby mirror. Richard wheeled to the mirror and broadly smiled when he saw his reflection. "You look very handsome!" Ashley exclaimed. "All of the girls will be chasing after you. If you want, you can wear that shirt to college on Monday," I said as I wrapped my arm around his shoulder. Richard said a loud, "Hmmm!" I loved seeing him that happy.

Ashley placed the shirt on Richard's tray. He likes to carry the items on his tray whenever we go shopping. Sometimes, I bring a large bag and hang it on the wheelchair's push bars. It's like using a shopping cart because it carries the items!

"Let's keep looking." Richard glanced at a white shirt. "Do you like that one?" The shirt had a cup of ramen noodles on the front with the word "Maruchan" written in big red letters. "This is a size large. Let's see if they have a medium," Ashley said as she searched through the shirts. "Extra large. Small. Small. Large. They don't have your size. Don't forget your birthday is coming up. You never know what the birthday fairy may bring you!" Richard grinned, which I believed was an "Oh, Aunt Ashley" grin.

"I saw one like this on Facebook," a nearby person said. I glanced in their direction. They spoke to someone who appeared to be the same age as Richard. When they mentioned Facebook, it made me ponder a few things. It made me think about how people react when I post Richard's photo on Facebook. They leave hundreds of likes and dozens of comments. Richard is called a "sweet baby," "handsome," "precious," and everything in between. You can only imagine what those comments say. These people do not know Richard personally. Some may have met him only once or twice.

People also comment, "Hi Richard!" or "I hope you have a great day today, Richard!" Those comments are lovely. However, I wish people would talk to Richard more than on a Facebook comment. I wish people would reach out and converse with him. I know the way

Richard communicates is unique. I also understand how people may fear the unknown. A lot of times, people don't know what to do. Maybe they don't know how to have a conversation with him. However, another part of me thinks it's not that hard. Including him is a great start.

When I read the Facebook comments to Richard, they always make him happy. I wish these comments were being said directly to him. Whenever we see someone we know, they greet Richard, but that's about it. Then, they have the rest of the conversation with me. It's really sad.

My train of thought broke when Richard raised his hand. "What is it?" He nudged the shirt that rested on his communication board. I moved it out of the way. Then Richard slowly spelled out "W," "A," "N," "T," "L," "I," "G," "H," "T," and "S," letter by letter. I had to concentrate when he did this because I didn't want to miss a letter. In my head, I always followed along with the words that he was spelling. "You want to go look for lights?" Richard nodded.

"He is over clothes shopping, Jamie! Let's go to the electronics," Ashley said as she took Richard's left hand. His fingers tightly gripped her hand. "Thank you," Richard said via his communication board. Ashley patted his shoulder. "You know I always have your back! I think you were getting bored hanging around us with our girl talk anyway." Richard nodded and smiled. He has such a polite way of getting his point across. I wish more people were like him.

I followed Ashley and Richard to the electronics section of the store. "Let's see if we can find what you want." A sign at the end of the aisle read "Electronics." Richard lit up as he rolled down the electronics aisle. He was always glad to do something, even if it was as simple as looking for lights.

A tall man stood close by. He looked to be about Richard's age. He turned to Richard and said, "Hey, are you looking for anything specific? I can help you reach what you need." My heart raced with excitement! This man was being so kind! Richard smiled as he nodded. "My name is Cameron. It is nice to meet you," Cameron said as he gazed down at Richard's tray. He noticed the communication board and understood its significance.

Ashley and I looked at each other. We were thinking the same thing. "I'm going to look over here and see if we can find something for your desk." "I'll make sure she picks nothing tacky," I said while pretending to look busy. Yes, we were giving Cameron and Richard space, but in reality, we were looking at them from the corner of our eyes! We rarely got to be a "fly on the wall" while my son showed out!

Richard smiled as he looked down at his tray. Cameron waited patiently while Richard slowly pointed to different letters on his communication board. I had no clue what he spelled.

"What are you looking for, Richard?" Cameron asked. Richard must have spelled his name. Richard gently continued to point to letter after letter. Cameron stood beside him and focused for several minutes. Meanwhile, Ashley and I looked through the various gadgets that were on display.

"You are looking for a monitor backlight. I know where those are. They are on a different aisle. Do you want to come with me? I can show you where they are." Richard moved his finger from one letter to another. It spelled a two-letter word. "He said go, Ashley. He said go," I whispered. Her jaw dropped. "Are you okay with me showing you where they are?" Cameron asked. Richard nodded and smiled brightly. Richard ditched us!

Richard pushed the joystick on his wheelchair and followed Cameron. "He won't see us follow him," Ashley whispered as she looked over her shoulder. I know she wanted to ensure that Richard was safe with a stranger. However, I wanted him to experience looking at things he enjoys with a guy close to his age. "Okay," I replied as we followed them.

Cameron retrieved something from the top shelf. He then stooped down beside Richard and held a black box before him. "How do these look?" Richard looked down and started to spell something.

A minute later, Cameron said, "Oh! You want blue. I think blue would look amazing!" He exchanged the boxes. "These lights connect to the back of your monitor. They also stick on and are powered by a USB port," Cameron explained as he held the box close to Richard. Richard smiled and pointed at the shelf. "What's up?" Richard looked down to spell something out. Cameron paid attention the entire time. He didn't seem to care that it took Richard a little while to respond. "Sure. I can get you one," Cameron replied as he grabbed another box.

Richard smiled as Cameron placed both boxes on his tray. "Is there anything else I can help with?" Richard shook his head and put his knuckle on a familiar section of his communication board. I knew Richard thanked him. "You are welcome! I'm down with computers and anything technology. I also enjoy customizing my computer setup. I understand where you are coming from," Cameron replied. I know hearing that had to make Richard feel invincible! I wished they could have become friends.

Richard smiled. I bet he wanted to answer more, but his tray was covered with boxes. "Let's find the ladies that were with you. Do you know where they are?" Richard shook his head. Ashley and I must have done well at staying out of sight! Cameron motioned for Richard to come toward the end of the aisle. Ashley and I pretended to walk up to them. "Hey guys!" "Hey," Cameron replied as Richard grinned. At that moment, Richard was glowing! "Did you find what you were looking for?" Ashley asked. Richard pointed to the boxes that rested over his communication board.

Suddenly, I got an idea! "I think Cameron would love your desk setup at home. Is it okay if I show him a picture?" Richard nodded. I scrolled through my camera roll and found a picture. "This is Richard's desk setup. He has two monitors." "Wow! Richard, you have the nicest desktop setup I've ever seen!" I know that compliment made Richard's day. No, that made his entire month!

"I love how you placed the lights around the top of the ceiling. I also like your desktop screen." Cameron didn't say anything about Richard's adaptive keyboard and mouse. Instead, he thought my son's stuff was incredible.

Cameron's kindness towards my son was significant. Many people feel uncomfortable when they converse with Richard. There is a lot of discussion about equity and connecting with those who are different. Unfortunately, this doesn't always result in a genuine understanding and acceptance of people's differences.

"I'm glad I could help you find the lights, Richard. They will look terrific!" "Thank you for helping," I said gratefully. "Anytime! Have a great rest of your day," Cameron replied as he grabbed something from the shelf.

I didn't want this moment to end, but it did. Cameron would never understand how much his kindness meant to us. When people like Cameron are kind to Richard in public, I call them "the saints in our day." The way Cameron treated Richard is a perfect example. His simple act of kindness added joy to our day because he thoughtfully offered to help. I'm not saying that we are entitled to anyone's help. However, we appreciate it!

Richard seemed more energized now compared to just a few minutes ago. I am learning so much about his need to interact with various people. College courses have been a great help with that. It is reassuring to see that other young people his age respect him. I have always worried about the impact of other people not understanding how and why Richard does things. The best thing is to get Richard out there and let him learn how to navigate life just like anyone else.

"Are you looking for anything else?" Richard shook his head. I bet he will want me to set his lights up later, and I will gladly do that for him! "Richard, do you need to make a bathroom stop?" Ashley asked. Believe it or not, all of Richard's aunts know how to care for him. They have seen me help him for many years, so they know what to do. Richard shook his head once more.

As we headed to the checkout lane, I remembered something Ashley told me long ago. She said, "There are a lot of spices in Richard's recipe." She referred to all of Richard's diagnoses as spices. They are what make him unique and extraordinary. I appreciated how she phrased that instead of saying he had many "problems." Ashley always knew how to make things better.

Surprisingly, we were next in line! An older gentleman was checking out just a few items. Ashley placed Richard's shirt and lights on the long checkout counter. She wrapped her arm around Richard and said, "It was good to see you today." The way she cares for him is extraordinary.

Before we knew it, the cashier, whose name tag read "Journei," reached for Richard's items. "Hello! Did you find everything you were looking for?" "This stuff isn't mine! It's Richard's." Journei looked at Richard. "My bad! Did you find everything you were looking for today, sir?" Richard nodded with a smile. "I'm glad. Those are some cool lights!" Journei replied as she scanned the shirt and lights. "I got this, Jamie," Ashley stated as she pulled out her credit card. "You don't have to do that! Let me get it!" I argued. Richard vocalized a loud "Mmm!" I was convinced he said, "Mine or me."

Richard reached for my purse, which held his wallet. I retrieved Richard's wallet from my Louis Vuitton purse and laid it on his tray. Richard opened his wallet and pointed to his credit card. "Well, aren't you just the man on the town? You are so grown. Next time, you should take us out to lunch," Ashley said as she handed Journei his credit card. Richard blushed. He was so embarrassed. I laughed! He can't take us anywhere!

"Enjoy the lights." Richard smiled as Journei placed his bag of items on his tray. "Have a good day, Journei." She handed back Richard's credit card. "You all do the same! Take care!" I smiled at my son. "I am going to put your wallet back in my purse where it is safe."

Ashley and I followed Richard as he rolled back outside. "It is always wonderful when I can see my bonus kid." Richard nudged his purchased items over. "I love you," he said via his communication board. Ashley kissed Richard's forehead. "I love you the most! Have a great rest of your day!" "Thanks for coming with us to shop! It's always fun having you around! I love you," I said as I hugged Ashley. "I love you more! See you soon!" Richard waved goodbye as she walked to her car.

I noticed nobody parked over the diagonal lines, so I considered that a win! I pressed the button, and we watched the van's side door slide open. Then, we waited for the van to lower. As expected, the ramp slowly extended and lowered. Richard rolled into his van.

"Are you ready to go home?" Richard hummed with approval. "Lucky for you, home is only a few minutes away." The tie-downs waited for me. I grabbed, pulled, and gave them a good tug.

Richard looked exhausted. Fortunately, we live in an area with everything nearby. I started the van and slowly backed out of the parking space.

CHAPTER FIVE

Richard gazed out the passenger window as we entered the main road. It won't be long until we are home, so I wanted him to enjoy every second. "I was just thinking this year has gone by so quickly. Your birthday is just around the corner. After that, it will be just a couple of months until Christmas. We will have to go for a drive and enjoy the lights! Remember the Christmas light road trip we took a few years ago? Maybe we could do another Christmas light road trip after you finish final exams this semester." Richard hummed with approval.

Christian worship music filled the van. I turned up the volume. Richard started to hum. If we can all just grasp and know that God is so mighty with how He loves and walks with us through every aspect of our lives, we cannot help but worship Him. Richard laughed aloud. There is just something extraordinary about watching Richard as he lives out his relationship with God. "God deserves our praise for all He does for us." Richard nodded and smiled! I reached across and grabbed his hand. We enjoyed a little "church" on our drive home.

When I am having an unimaginable difficult time with Richard, my favorite Bible verse to depend on is Psalm 121:1. That Bible verse says, "I lift up my eyes to the hills. From where does my help come from? My help comes from the LORD, the Maker of heaven and earth." That Bible verse assures me that I am never alone.

In any situation, I know that God is always on the throne. Even when I can't find out what is troubling Richard, God is on the throne. Even when Richard yells in pain, God is on the throne. Even in our darkest hour, God is on the throne. God's name is above any diagnosis or heartbreak because He is the healer of a broken heart. God's love and strength will restore you and make you perfect and complete, needing nothing. So, every morning, I pray, "God, let me be your light bearer. Do what only you can do in me."

I made a right turn and drove down our quiet neighborhood street. I love our neighborhood. It's a tree-lined street where each home features a unique architectural style. Our home is a two-story colonial with a modern design. I love our dual master suites and the indoor and outdoor open spaces. There is ample space for me to work on the second floor while Richard makes himself comfortable on the first floor.

Richard smiled as I parked the van in the garage. "Did you have a good time?" Richard nodded. "I'm glad! I'm turning you loose," I said as I unfastened the tie-downs. Richard hysterically laughed as he rolled down the ramp. I grabbed the to-go boxes and chopsticks and stacked them on Richard's tray.

"Thank you for helping me carry these things inside. Here are your keys." I placed the keys on his cluttered tray. Richard looked down and pressed his right knuckle on the button. The ramp raised and slid in before the sliding door shut.

I opened the door, and Richard rolled to the kitchen. "I'm going to lighten your load," I said as I put the leftovers into the fridge. Richard gestured toward the remaining items stacked on his tray. "We can go put that away."

We made our way down the long hallway and into Richard's room. "You probably need to go to the bathroom by now." He nodded. I placed his chopsticks, new shirt, and monitor lights on his desk. Richard raised his arms as I detached his tray and set it aside. He then wheeled into his bathroom.

When this house was built, I designed it to meet Richard's needs. His spacious en-suite bathroom allows two people to move around freely. His sink is lowered and has an open space provided so he can roll his wheelchair right up to the sink. Grab bars are attached to Richard's toilet to help ensure his safety. He also has a "roll-in" shower with a shower chair!

I unfastened Richard's seat belt and placed his feet on the ground. "Are you ready?" I bent my knees and put my right arm around his back. Richard placed his arms around my neck, leaned forward, and pushed with his legs. I carefully guided him as he stood up. He then started to lean on me. "You got this. Please stand up." I placed my left hand on his side. "Turn with me." Richard slowly turned around. "Don't sit down just yet." I pulled everything down and helped lower him onto the toilet.

Richard rested his arms on the toilet's grab bars. I stood behind his electric wheelchair and moved the joystick. I slowly drove it out of the bathroom, turned it off, and plugged it in. I always made sure to charge Richard's electric wheelchair after each outing.

Richard smiled as I rolled his manual wheelchair into the bathroom and locked the wheels. I know this process may seem awkward, but we are used to it. I avoid making a big deal out of it because I never want to embarrass Richard.

I grabbed some toilet paper and did what I needed to do. Richard wrapped his arms around my neck. I placed my right arm around his back. "On three. One. Two. Three." Richard stood up. Then I buttoned his pants. "Let's turn back the other way." Richard hummed in agreement. I put my left arm around him. During transfers, I always say what to do. That way, Richard wouldn't try to move when I wasn't ready. It helps us move simultaneously, which helps keep things safe.

Richard slowly shifted his feet. "Turn. Turn. Catch your balance," I instructed as I held onto him. "Are you good?" Richard hummed. "Please sit down." I guided him back into his wheelchair.

Richard smiled as I unlocked his wheels and rolled him to the sink. I pulled out a clean washcloth, soaked it with warm water, and handed it to him. Richard sighed. "You can do it. You are in no hurry." I could tell Richard was tired and wanted me to wash his face. However, I knew that he could do this himself.

The fundamental principle in caregiving for individuals with exceptionalities is to promote their self-help skills as much as possible. When children are continually catered to and are not given expectations toward development, they will spend their lives wallowing in learned helplessness. From the outside, some may think it looks like being mean and pushing beyond capabilities. Children who are given high expectations and then partner with others to reach those expectations will grow up to be high achievers. In Richard's situation, I always ask him to do things I know he can do.

Richard used both hands to scrub his face as I washed my hands. When he finished, Richard turned his head toward me and smiled. "I know you are tired. Do you want to change out of those pants?" Richard shook his head. "Do you want to change your shirt?" He shook his head again. I would want to sleep in something more comfortable if it were me. Maybe Richard is too tired to deal with changing his clothes. It's times like this when I let him decide because he can in this situation. I try to promote his independence as much as possible. At the end of the day, he is a grown man. If he decides to stay in his jeans, then so be it.

I didn't fasten Richard's seat belt only because he was about to transfer back out of his wheelchair. "Please pick your feet up. Hands and feet in the ride at all times!" Richard laughed as he did. There are many times when I make him laugh on purpose.

I pushed Richard back into his room and over beside the bed. "That was a long drive." Richard covered his face and chortled! I grabbed the remote and lowered his bed. We were about to go through the same process again. Next, I locked his wheelchair. Richard placed his feet on the floor before I bent down. I wrapped my right arm around his back and put my left hand on his side. Then he placed his arms around my neck. "Ready. Set. Stand up." I assisted Richard to his feet. "Please turn one more time. It's a great exercise to have you do two transfers in a row," I said as I steadied his balance. We turned toward the bed. "You are there. Please sit down." Richard slowly bent his knees. After he sat on the bed, I ensured his feet were flat on the floor.

I elevated the head of the bed and put my hand on Richard's left shoulder to help him balance. Then, I placed my left arm behind his back and my right arm under his knees. In one swift, rotating motion, I laid him down. I'm incredibly grateful that he isn't heavy. My body has grown accustomed to moving him. Over the years, my muscles became stronger as Richard continued to grow.

Richard rested on his back as I removed his shoes. "I'm going to get you a fresh pair of socks." He hummed with approval. Richard has poor circulation, which causes his toes to feel cold. I grabbed a pair of black socks from his dresser. When I returned to the bed, I noticed goosebumps all over his arms. "I know you're cold. Please hang on." I removed his current pair of socks and added a fresh pair. Then I pulled the covers over him. "Is that better?" Richard smiled.

"Are you going to fall asleep soon?" Richard shook his head. "Are you going to fight going to sleep?" Richard smirked mischievously. Richard resists sleep and likes to stay up late because he knows other people his age do the same thing. I allow him because it is a choice he can independently make. Richard is a grown man and deserves to make his own decisions. Despite all of this, he still takes a daily nap because he knows his body needs rest.

"Get some sleep. I am going in the living room for a while," I said as I kissed Richard's forehead. Richard grinned from ear to ear.

CHAPTER SIX

I walked to the living room and sat on the couch. Then I checked my phone and tapped the website link where one of Richard's birthday gifts waited. I'm thinking about buying Richard a ring for his birthday because I saw him looking at rings online a few months ago. I playfully teased him by saying he had a secret girlfriend he intended to marry. Richard informed me that he wanted a ring since he never had one. He also mentioned he liked the rings he saw his college classmates wearing.

The ring that I think he will love is made of tungsten with a blue metallic finish. It also includes a layer of gray metal that rests on top of the blue metal. I believe Richard would pick this design out himself!

After that, I decided to check my Facebook. That reminded me of when someone on Facebook commented, "Richard is always happy! I have never seen him without a smile on his face." Yes, I only post about good times on Facebook. Many people adore Richard on social media. However, they are unaware of the harsh reality of things. They are oblivious to the darker side of reality, which is a dismal chamber filled with sadness.

Nobody knows about the sleepless nights. Nobody knows about our miscommunications. Nobody knows about Richard's pain in his back, knees, legs, neck, and arms. Nobody knows how hard I try to keep him happy. Nobody knows about the harsh reality that we face. People don't see my heartache as I struggle to find out what he wants. They don't see me crying ugly tears behind closed doors. They have no idea, and I prefer it that way. It's not their responsibility to know.

Few people have a fundamental understanding of what it takes to be a caregiver, let alone a parent to someone with many obstacles to overcome. The heartbreak, denial, why God, and eventual acceptance that occurs upon learning about your child's diagnosis is something many do not understand.

At first, there is heartache. Later, that heartache morphs into a perspective of doing whatever is possible to help your child live a productive life and sometimes just survive. Along your journey, you pray, collaborate with parent groups, research the latest therapy techniques, and devise a plan of action with specialists.

If you have not walked this journey, you have no idea about the rough nights. Think of how you cradled your infant the first time they dealt with an illness. Recall the trepidations that flooded your heart about whether you were doing the right thing for your child. For me, this never ends. I always experience these trepidations. Nobody knows how I struggle to guess what Richard wants when he can't tell me. Nobody experiences Richard's pain in his back, legs, neck, and arms. Nobody understands the sharp pain in my heart when I cannot alleviate his chronic pain. Nobody knows the devastation I felt when I learned Richard has limited vision. The list goes on and on.

Many nights after Richard went to sleep, I fell to my knees and prayed. I asked, "God, why must Richard experience the challenges he goes through?" In a still, small voice, God spoke into my heart and said, "My grace is sufficient."

Over the years, I've changed my prayers from why to how. I now ask, "God, how do You want me to handle this situation? How are You using this situation to help me grow? How do You want me to be more like You?"

Now, there are times when I privately have my own pity party. I never let Richard see me in my moments of weakness. However, this is when my close friends help lift me up. Staying focused on building my spiritual relationship through prayer, praise, and worship is one of the most valuable avenues toward emotional strength. Surrounding myself with others who share my faith has pulled me forward when I felt everything sliding downhill. These people have been my biggest supporters and listening ears as I work toward being an advocate for my son and others. I have been honored to come alongside so many who find themselves in this unique place of honor. God works everything out for the good of those who are called according to His purpose.

I know that I'm not alone because everyone faces obstacles in life. These may include financial difficulties, health concerns, unemployment, separation, or academic challenges. We all deal with something. That's life. I've learned to focus on the positive things. Believe it or not, there is always something good in every situation. You just have to look for it. If you do, you will find something good!

The Bible says there will always be trouble and problems, but there is always something to be thankful for! I am grateful that Richard is not in and out of the hospital. He is overall healthy and doing well. Richard is working towards greater independence and is taking college courses. He is playing the cards that life dealt to him like a pro! I am incredibly proud of him!

When I look at Richard, I see his strength! Cerebral palsy does not define him. It is only something he deals with. Richard is a young man who enjoys technology, dining out, and socializing. He is just like everybody else! However, I want so much more for him. I want Richard to broaden his life by being more involved in various activities. Unfortunately, there are no day programs that would meet his needs. Our small community has few options, but we travel to activities when possible.

Some have questioned my decision to homeschool Richard. For us, it was the right decision. When Richard was five, I was informed that he would never learn to read because he couldn't speak. Well, Richard read right at the same time developmental specialists expected him to! My mom and I always believed in him when nobody else did.

Socialization and interpersonal skills are big concerns of those who don't support homeschooling. I see no issues for Richard in these areas. From the earliest years, he interacted with a variety of people. I started Richard out with a "Mommy and Me" group that was sponsored by our therapy group. Between Richard's church friends, aunts, cousins, and a whole group of therapy friends, he has learned the give and take of relationships. I pray Richard can make friends that he can keep. Cameron would have made a great friend. He would be the kind of guy Richard would enjoy spending time with. I want a lot of things for my son. However, I've learned that everything I want is not always possible or doesn't happen when I want it to. That was a hard lesson to learn.

After all that thinking, I decided it was time to check on Richard. I tiptoed down the hall and peeked into his room. Richard was sound asleep. I hoped he was getting plenty of rest. Then I took another good look at him. As Richard gets older, he looks more and more like his dad, Robert. Richard inherited his deep brown eyes and black curly hair from him.

I met Robert in college. We started dating at the beginning of my freshman year. Since I thought we were in love, I decided to allow our relationship to move to a physical level. In hindsight, that was not the best decision.

When I learned that I was pregnant, I felt I needed to tell Robert so we could make plans for our future. I thought everything would be perfect and that we would become a family. However, Robert wanted nothing to do with me at that point. I had never felt rejection like that before. Robert hurt me as he walked away without ever looking back. It is his loss because he never got to be the dad of a remarkable young man.

After Robert and I split up, I was deeply wounded. I felt betrayed and thrown to the side as if I had done something wrong. I spent many hours weeping about the whole situation. Then I read in the book of Hebrews about the "root of bitterness." I was enlightened to understand that this is what I had allowed to happen in my heart. It took time and a lot of effort, but I forgave Robert.

At this time, I leaned heavily on God and my family. I was 20 when I gave birth to Richard. My mom was there to support me through it all. I was overjoyed to welcome my son into the world! Meanwhile, Robert's family still lived in our town. The news spread, and his family learned about Richard's cerebral palsy. Robert's mom sent me a card and wrote how sorry she was that my baby was diagnosed with cerebral palsy. In the meantime, I never heard from Robert. He never tried to be involved in Richard's life.

When Richard was eight, he asked about his dad. He heard the kids in his Sunday school class discuss their dads' jobs. They were learning about how Jesus' earthly dad was a carpenter. Richard asked where his dad was. I told him I didn't know, and it had been many years since I had seen him.

Early elementary ages seem to be when children become curious about family dynamics and why their family may differ from those around them. When talking to your child, you must be honest and tailor your response to the child's age and understanding. Give them time to process the information and ask more questions.

At another time, Richard asked if his dad loved him. I told him that his dad never met him and did not know what a wonderful person he was. Other than that, Richard never brought up his dad. He seems content without a dad because he knows I love him enough for two parents combined!

Speaking of dads, I wish my dad were still alive. I was 17 when my dad passed away from cancer. When Dad knew he had little time left, he told me he wanted me to take over his business. He informed me that he felt I could work in the field based on the areas I excelled at in school. Dad also wanted me to be financially stable after he was gone.

Prior to his passing, Dad hired an interim CEO to oversee the business' growth and development. After graduation, I went to college and worked part-time at the business. I started at the bottom and worked my way up while being a single mom in college. That was very difficult, but it was worth the investment in my personal development. Nearly a decade later, when the interim CEO was ready to retire, I took over the business and became the CEO!

I know my dad would be proud of me. More importantly, I know he would have loved Richard and been wonderful with him. Dad would have served as a role model for Richard to look up to. Life would have been different if he were still here. I thank God for having him in my life for 17 years. Dad knew where his true treasures were and worked hard to help me understand that. It was the strength that he showed in the face of great trials that has helped me to stand firm in difficult situations.

My mom often tells me how much my dad wanted the best for me. Mom was beyond devastated by my dad's passing. I heard her crying in her room when she thought I wouldn't hear. I also witnessed her cry out to God in prayer. God answered those prayers through a harrowing journey, but that is her story to tell.

Richard's iPad chimed. He received a message from Ashley. Once he wakes up, he can read the text. Richard's peers love to text, and Richard is no exception. Since the standard phone is more difficult for him to navigate, we use an iPad as his phone.

I will often text Richard throughout the day when he is with caregivers. I ask how his day is, if he is okay, or if he wants me to pick up dinner. Many of Richard's responses are one or two words. That is because it is so time-consuming for him to spell out a response. His caregivers work with him to send his texts. Richard uses his communication board to spell what he wants to text. Then, the caregiver types out the sentence before reading it back to him. It is a long process, but those thoughts are Richard's. That makes it all worth it.

I sometimes feel emotional when I receive a complete sentence from Richard because there is no communication barrier between us. Receiving a longer text has made me tear up, and I hated it when it made me cry. For the past 23 years, I kept telling myself I would get used to this. I never have.

As Richard's mom, I know caring for him is a life-long endeavor. There will never be a magic pill that will cure his level of cerebral palsy. Richard can have an accessible van, a great crew of caregivers, a mom who loves him, an accessible home, and the best adaptive equipment he can use. But is it enough? Is he truly happy? Does he think he is living a fulfilled and meaningful life? I hope so.

Once Richard started taking college courses, I noticed a significant change in his self-confidence. It was difficult for me to let him go to college. Ultimately, I must remember that Richard can manage for himself in many ways. It is the physical challenges that require him to have assistance.

Overall, Richard appears happy most of the time. Every day, I check to see how he is doing.

I take his mental health seriously because I don't want him to get depressed. Thankfully, Richard has never shown any signs of depression.

There is so much that I can't control in Richard's life. Yes, I am his mom, but I do not have all the control I want. If it were up to me, he would have loads of friends. He would get invited to many events. He would invite his friends to his own home. I know I can't control others or make them Richard's friends. So, in the meantime, I will do what I can control. I will check on him and give him everything he needs. I will treat him with the respect that he deserves. I will take him places in hopes of him meeting someone. I will allow his aunts to continue to shower him with love. I can only do what I can control.

Real love is never easy. Over the years, I've learned to adapt to any situation. That means I meet Richard where he is and do anything he needs. I will always be Richard's biggest fan and support him in anything he wants to try.

I walked back to the living room and laid on the couch. All of a sudden, a notification from Julie popped up on my phone. Julie is my other best friend! She is also another one of Richard's aunts! Julie's text read, "Jamie! I have the best birthday present in mind for Richard! How about a massage chair? We can all pay for it. The massage chair can be from all of us. Richard will love it! His muscles will thank us!" It took all my willpower not to let out a sound of excitement!

My heart was so moved that my jaw dropped! I replied that I thought it was an excellent idea. I adored how thoughtful my best friends were toward Richard. The massage chair would benefit Richard's body. His muscles get so tight that it hurts his back, legs, knees, neck, arms, and wrists. There is plenty of room for a massage chair in his room. I know Richard will want to use it all the time!

Taking care of Richard's body is crucial. After he was discharged from occupational and physical therapy, he was assigned a home exercise maintenance program. That means Richard continues to do his therapy at home. This program helps his body stay the same and not regress. During the week, Richard exercises with a caregiver. Exercise is essential for anyone. However, it is vital for individuals with cerebral palsy. Exercise can keep their muscles in check! It can help prevent their muscles from getting tighter and weaker.

Richard has his own way of exercising! He stands for an entire minute with assistance. After taking a break, he repeats the process several times to keep his legs strong. Additionally, Richard uses weighted wrist wraps to improve his shoulder strength and balance by raising them in the air. Richard also operates an arm bike to strengthen his upper body. He has built the strength needed to utilize the handrims on his manual wheelchair. Our long hallway makes a great practice track for him!

Richard also has a royal blue platform walker! The walker has armrests that hold his arms in place. Richard places his arms on the armrests before him, then wraps his hands around the grip bars. As Richard walks, a caregiver or I walk behind him and hold onto his gait belt.

Richard usually walks our long hallway five times a week to maintain his endurance and strength. That keeps his legs strong and allows him to transfer easily. If Richard stopped walking and exercising, he would become weaker, making transfers and movements more difficult.

Besides exercising, Richard receives Botox injections every six months to help relax his muscles. He also takes baclofen daily and gets plenty of rest. A massage chair would be a great addition to the mix! I couldn't think of a better birthday present to get him this year!

Richard requires a lot of care. That is by no means a secret. There was a time when my neighbor asked me a harsh question. They asked, "You are not getting any younger. Caring for Richard must wear on you mentally and physically. So, why don't you put Richard in a group home or nursing home?" I understand how some families choose to go those routes. Everyone's situation is different. People handle and solve things differently. I will respect others' decisions because I do not know their circumstances.

However, I will never put Richard in a nursing home or group home. He will live with me as long as I'm alive. I also know there will be a day when I will be too old to lift him. When I reach that point, I will hire more help. I am also aware that Richard will outlive me. Life expectancy for people with cerebral palsy can be well into the 70s!

Another question people asked me was, "Are you going to have more kids?" I decided that Richard should be an only child because I knew he would need a lot of care. In the past, my brain would come up with scenarios. Let's pretend that my other son has a football game. However,

Richard and I won't be able to come because Richard is not feeling well. I don't want my other child to resent Richard for receiving most of the attention, nor do I want him to be upset with Richard for something he cannot control.

I believe Richard would love having someone else around, but I make sure to have realistic judgment. I will not pretend or assume that Richard and his brother or sister would be best friends. I know how stubborn teenagers can be because they have their own way of thinking. Siblings can get jealous of each other. That usually happens if one gets more attention than the other. It can lead to disagreements between the two. However, some kids are also very mature and understanding. It's all a gamble. You don't know what kind of child you will end up with. As hard as it was, I decided not to have another child.

I've also made other choices for my life. I know I was young when I had Richard. There were plenty of opportunities to develop other relationships after Robert. I was so deeply hurt for a long time before I came to the place of forgiveness. Over the years, I've had a few dates but no serious relationships. I decided my focus needed to be on developing my career and caring for Richard. It's not that I am opposed to being in a relationship. It just isn't something I am actively pursuing.

Now, some people do not always ask me difficult questions. Instead, they complement me! I feel so blessed, yet unworthy when they do. I was told that I am a wonderful mom to Richard. For the most part, I think I am. I know how I handle things may differ from the next parent. My situations, priorities, and insights as a mom may vary from the parent standing beside me. You cannot compare apples to oranges.

I'm not perfect, and I will call myself out! I know that I'm a helicopter mom! I am trying to learn how to give Richard space. It's tough to balance how much I need to be around. Richard has a break from me when he is with a caregiver. The caregivers are good at promoting Richard's independence. They give him space to make decisions for himself and let him control what he can.

For the most part, Richard is easygoing. I'm grateful that he handles his challenges with patience and tenacity. However, there have been some challenging times. I won't claim that my son is perfect because nobody is flawless.

You can bet your top dollar that Richard has his moments. We all do! Sometimes, Richard is in a bad mood because he can't get comfortable or his back hurts. I always try to be patient as I figure out what is wrong.

However, there are also days when he acts extra on purpose! Richard puts my patience to the test! There are times when Richard argues and disagrees with me. He crosses his arms, shoots me a stare, and his voice is more agitated. His hums are deeper and less pleasant-sounding. We all can have disagreements, and Richard is no exception.

Richard doesn't argue with me very often. When he does, we always talk things through. I ask what is bothering him and take time to figure it out. If Richard acted ugly, he would always apologize. He does that by making a sweet humming sound or taking my hand.

Even on tough days, I never raise my voice or yell at Richard. Instead, I give him space. Those days are hard. However, it's going to be alright. The bad times have made me appreciate the good times. All the good memories make up for it. Real love is never easy. You must love someone at all times, unconditionally, even on their bad days.

I decided to check my Facebook to shift my thoughts away from negative things. That didn't last long. Welcome to the part of my life that nobody knows about. I saw a post about someone's son getting engaged. Don't get me wrong, I am extremely happy for him, but it just makes me sad for Richard. He has never had a girlfriend or experienced his first kiss. Richard is such a wonderful person. I pray people can see him for who he truly is instead of someone who needs care and uses a wheelchair.

I redirected my thoughts to a memory of Richard and his Aunt Ashley. There was a time when Ashley asked Richard if he wanted a girlfriend. He didn't answer. However, she kept asking him. Richard broadly grinned while he attempted to cover his face. What came out of Ashley's mouth next surprised me. She asked, "Would you want a girlfriend who uses a wheelchair too?" Richard blushed as he nodded. Then I asked, "What if a girl didn't use a wheelchair but showed she liked you? Would you date her?" Richard nodded again. At that moment, I discovered he thought about that part of his life.

After that, I told Richard that when he got a girlfriend, I would cook dinner so they could have their date in our dining room. Richard loved that idea! I then asked if he would also like to watch a movie with her. He nodded with a bright smile.

It is important for Richard to feel confident and have a well-developed sense of self-worth. I never focus on his flaws. Instead, I always empower him! I thank God that Richard has good self-esteem. I tell Richard that he is handsome, and he has never disagreed. I hope Richard knows he is worthy of a young woman's love. If he tells me he likes a girl, I will encourage him to go get her! I never want to put limitations on my son. He deserves just as much as everyone else! God created Richard as a unique and worthy individual. No one has the right to make him out to be any less than that!

CHAPTER SEVEN

I walked back into Richard's room to check on him. He greeted me with a cheerful hum. "Hey, sweetheart. I didn't know you woke up. You should have called for me." Richard smiled as he stretched his arms. "Do you feel like taking a shower?" He nodded. "I'm going to get your nightclothes." I gathered Richard's favorite soft red T-shirt for sleeping, black socks, pajama pants, and boxers.

"Aunt Ashley texted you while you were asleep. Would you like to see what she said?" Richard grinned. I took his iPad and opened the messaging app. "Aunt Ashley said that she had a great time seeing you today! She also said that she loves you. Do you want to text her back?" Richard nodded. "Do you want me to help you send the text? Or do you want to spell out what you want to say?" I always wanted to give him a choice when I could. Richard pointed at me. "How about you tell her that you love her? You can also add that you were happy to see her." Richard nodded. As I sent the text, I wondered if that's what he wanted to say in his message. What if he just agreed to make things easier? There are some things that I will never know.

"Are you ready?" Richard motioned toward the bed's remote. I laughed and raised the head of the bed. "You are funny." I removed Richard's socks to prevent him from slipping when he stood up. Then, I helped him bend his knees. "Please turn your head and body toward me. Lean this way." I placed my left hand behind his right shoulder and helped Richard roll onto his side. After that, I put my right hand under the bend of his knees. "Please do your best to push yourself up with your right arm." I know this part is always hard for Richard. However, I continue to encourage him to try. I positioned my left arm underneath him and brought his legs to the side of the bed. Next, I lifted and moved him into a sitting position. I put my arm around Richard and lowered the bed until his feet touched the floor.

I glanced down at Richard's wheelchair. I always check to ensure the wheels are locked before transferring him. There was a time when

I didn't check. It was a complete disaster! When I tried to transfer Richard to his wheelchair, it gradually kept rolling away! I was terrified because there was no one else around to help! By the grace of God, I eventually got Richard into his wheelchair. I learned a crucial lesson that day!

Richard leaned forward and placed his cheek against mine. "I love you." He softly hummed in response. I love the gentleness in his voice. I find it interesting how basic emotions can be expressed in the simplest ways. It does not matter how simple it is because it is just as meaningful.

Richard wrapped his arms around my neck. I placed my hands on his back and side. "On three. One. Two. Three." I helped him to his feet. "Let's turn." I guided Richard to step in front of his wheelchair. Richard has the strength to stand and step. However, he can't maintain his balance by himself. "Have a seat." I guided him into the wheelchair. Richard smiled as he picked up his feet. I rolled him into his bathroom and locked the wheels.

Richard's accessible shower is on the right side of the bathroom. It is spacious enough to accommodate two people. I gently took Richard's right arm and pushed it through his shirt's armhole. His elbows are usually bent, so that armhole gets stretched out every time! I raised the shirt over his head, and it slid off his left arm with no trouble. It is always easier to remove a shirt than to put one on.

I positioned the shower chair next to Richard's wheelchair and locked it. His shower chair is a waterproof plastic wheelchair with armrests and wheels. Richard wrapped his arms around my neck. "Ready to do it all over again?" He laughed. "One. Two. Three. Please stand up." I helped him to his feet. Richard has come a long way when it comes to his transfers. When he was young, I used to have to lift him entirely. I knew he would not stay small forever, so we worked hard until transferring got easier.

"Turn to your left." Richard shuffled, turned, and stood in front of the shower chair. With one hand, I pulled everything down. "You can have a seat." I helped lower Richard into his shower chair. "Are you comfortable?" He nodded.

Richard laughed as I tossed his clothes into the nearby laundry basket. "Do you think it is funny that I have more laundry to do?" I put on my bathrobe. When I bathe Richard, I always wear a robe to prevent my clothes from getting wet and to cover myself completely. I fastened the shower chair's seat belt, removed my shoes, and turned on the shower. "Who's ready?" Richard grinned.

I slowly rolled him in and pulled the shower curtain. "No cold water for you!" I grabbed the showerhead, turned it away from Richard, and turned on the water. We have a hand-held showerhead, which makes it easy to bathe Richard without getting wet! With the water warmed up, I allowed it to run over his right leg. Richard's body became rigid as the water touched his skin. "You are all good." Richard closed his eyes and smiled.

Then, I soaked a washcloth and placed it on his leg. Richard let out an audible sigh. I hope this shower helps alleviate some of his pain.

"Since I washed your hair yesterday, we won't wash it today." Richard nodded as I grabbed his mahogany teakwood body wash. He loves the way it smells! I applied the body wash onto the washcloth and handed it to Richard. He slowly cleaned his left hand.

I've worked hard to help Richard be as independent as possible. However, it was not always that way. I was so afraid to let anyone touch him. I didn't want anything bad to happen to him. As Richard got older, I learned how important it was to allow him to try and fail. I realized that I could not protect him from negative situations and consequences as these are part of the necessary steps everyone goes through as they grow up.

Richard washed his right hand. I am very proud that he can do that himself. When he was finished, he handed the washcloth to me. I cleaned Richard's right leg. He relaxed as I moved to his other leg.

Then, Richard blinked rapidly. He does this when he has something in his eye. "Please look up." I placed my thumb on his right lower eyelid. I saw nothing. So, I checked his other eye and noticed an eyelash stuck in the corner. I easily removed it. "Does that feel better?" Richard smiled and rubbed his left eye.

I applied body wash to the washcloth and took Richard's right foot. I cleaned the top, between the toes, and the bottom of his foot. Then, I repeated the same process for his left foot.

Richard held his right arm out as I added more body wash to the washcloth. I took his arm and sprayed it with warm water. Then, I cleaned it from front to back. Richard extended his left arm. "After we get done, do you want to get on your computer?" Richard smiled. "That is a great plan."

Richard lifted his arms as I cleaned his armpits. "Please lean forward." He leaned forward as I washed his shoulders. His shoulder muscles felt tight. That made me even more excited for his massage chair to come!

During this shower, I paid close attention to make sure that I saw zero pressure sores. People with limited mobility are more susceptible to pressure sores and skin rashes. If you sit or lie in one position for an extended period, you may develop sores. Pressure sores can be painful and take weeks to heal. Thankfully, Richard has never had one.

I took Richard's hands and checked his fingernails. They were clean and short. "You are all set." An urgent grunt escaped Richard's lips as I turned off the water. "What is wrong?" Richard's eyes stared at me. I had no idea what was wrong.

There are times when Richard's inability to communicate stings my heart. If only I could know what he was thinking. Many times, I am limited to reading his body language. Richard's thoughts are like treasures stored in a vault that not even the best locksmith can break inside. If only I could find a way to help Richard share his treasures.

There have been difficult days in the past. I remind myself that during every bad moment, another happy memory awaits. The bad moment is only temporary, and it always ends.

During Richard's journey, there were moments when I felt afraid. I was uncertain about what to do or how to help him. Most of the care I have done comes out of guessing what will work. I attempt to make sense of what Richard is trying to communicate without the words to do so. I've been at a place where fear overwhelmed me. However, I discovered a valuable lesson along the way. I realized that there is no fear in the place of love. That's right! There is no fear in the place of love!

I do my best to make communication accessible for Richard. I achieve this by asking yes or no questions he can answer by nodding or shaking his head. Additionally, I have provided him with a communication board featuring bold letters that he can easily see. I am committed to meeting Richard's communication needs.

Most importantly, I will meet Richard where he is able! Unfortunately, some days are very unclear communication-wise. However, some days are so amazing that they shake my heart and bring me to my knees!

When there is a communication barrier between us, I just believe. I cannot tell you how often I wondered if Richard felt a certain way. I've felt uncertain about many things because he cannot tell me. What gets me the most is not knowing how much he loves me. From a mother's perspective, that isn't easy. Richard never had a way to fully express his love for me or convey his thoughts about me. The unknown hurts, but I've learned to believe he loves me just as much.

We are used to hearing words for confirmation. We want to hear something to know that it is true. It doesn't work that way with Richard. Over the years, I vowed to find a way for him to express his thoughts thoroughly. However, reality won, and I've learned to accept that.

There are times when love is not expressed with words. It can be shown through body language! There have been miraculous times between Richard and I. There were moments when we looked into each other's eyes, and I could feel his love. There are days when Richard is glad to see me and greets me with a radiant smile! Moments like that make me feel invincible! Whenever I have doubts, I rely on the good times for support. That is how I understand his true feelings in my heart. During tough times, love always triumphs in the end. Love prevails because it is always there, no matter what. The assurance of love stands on solid ground. It cannot be shaken!

In an instant, I realized what was wrong. Richard knows he is about to get out of the shower and feel cold. "Are you upset that you are about to get cold?" Richard tensed up and nodded. So, that is what he was thinking about! I rarely get it spot-on like that!

I grabbed a towel and wrapped it around him. "Is that any better?" Richard shook his head and sighed deeply at me. "I'm so sorry." I grabbed another towel and dried him off.

I pulled back the shower curtain and rolled Richard out. I then angled the shower chair and locked its wheels. "Let me get your clothes." I removed my bathrobe and retrieved his clothes. Richard will be happier once he gets dressed!

As I walked back into the bathroom, Richard extended his right arm. I gently took his arm and placed it through the right armhole. Then I put the shirt over his head and gently moved his left arm through the other armhole.

I slid Richard's boxers and pajama pants over each leg. I refrained from putting on his socks so he could have a better grip. "I know you are ready." I unbuckled the shower chair's seat belt.

Richard wrapped his arms around my neck. I knew he was ready to get on his computer, but he had to wait to finish getting dressed. I knew none of this was fun for him. I placed my arm around his back and my other hand on his side. Richard leaned forward. "One. Two. Three. You got it," I said as he stood up.

I pulled Richard's boxers and pajama pants up and held him with my other arm. Now, that takes skill! "We are turning to the right." Richard slowly pivoted. "You are there. Have a seat." I helped Richard into his wheelchair. He grinned. "There we go. That's how we do it!" I fastened the wheelchair's seat belt and put his socks and house shoes on each foot. Richard's feet felt cold due to poor circulation. Hopefully, his house shoes will warm them up.

I wheeled Richard back into his room. He raised his arms as I attached the tray for his manual wheelchair. Richard has two wheelchair trays: one for his electric wheelchair and one for his manual wheelchair. Each tray features a large laminated communication board.

"Where are your splints?" Richard looked at his desk. "Did Kekoa put them in the drawer?" He nodded. "Did you think I wouldn't be able to find them?" Richard chuckled and held out his left hand. I gently placed his hand into the blue splint and fastened it with the Velcro straps. Richard smiled as I did the same thing for his right hand.

Richard tightened his grip on the handrims and gradually maneuvered himself to his desk. Richard's desk is left without an office chair because his wheelchair serves as an office chair! I'm thankful that he has a remarkably nice manual wheelchair. Mr. David, the gentleman who came to complete Richard's wheelchair evaluation, listened to all of my concerns. The mobility company was able to design and build his wheelchair within six months!

I take excellent care of Richard's wheelchair. It is like taking care of a vehicle! I deep-cleaned his wheelchair last weekend while he was taking a nap. I clean it once a month, sometimes twice a month. I always make sure my son is rolling in style!

"Let's straighten you up so you can see." I re-adjusted Richard's wheelchair. We never completely push Richard up to his desk. If we did, he couldn't access his communication board. I placed his cordless keyboard and computer mouse on his tray. Richard glanced up at his giant computer monitors.

Richard's room and desk setup are like no other! The walls are light gray, and the room is shaped like a giant square. Richard's bed and closet are on the right side, while his desk is on the left. There is a massive LED light strip that wraps entirely around the ceiling. You can change the color of the lights, but Richard prefers to keep the color setting on bright blue. He also has a blue lava lamp on the left side of his desk. We usually leave the lights off in Richard's room so he can enjoy his lights.

Richard also has a large black L-shaped desk that measures five by three feet. It provides enough space for Richard and someone else to sit beside and assist him. Two large computer monitors are also placed side by side on his desk. I am thankful that he can easily see them.

Richard pointed to the card on his desk. "You have to sign Seraphina's birthday card!" The lights in Richard's room reflected off of his wheelchair's blue frame. It was a stunning sight because everything was glowing, including the grin on his face! "I know you will be happy to put this in the mail. All you need to do is write your name."

I placed a pen in Richard's right hand and held the card in place. Richard held the pen vertically and grasped it with his fingers. He moved his hand as a giant "R" appeared on the card. Then he went for his "I." Richard never picked up the pen, so the "I" was written on top of the "R." Richard writes his letters large and squiggly. However, I do not care how his handwriting looks. I'm proud that he can write his name. It took him years to learn how to do that.

"Remember what LD told you," I kindly reminded him as I tapped the card. Richard lifted his hand and moved it over. That will help keep his letters from stacking on top of each other.

During his occupational therapy sessions, Richard worked with an outgoing young woman. LD, the nickname the clinic gave her, is around 26 years old. Her real name is a little hard to pronounce because she is from Romania! Richard adored her and thought she was hilarious! He would laugh a lot when he was with her. She made going to therapy fun for him. LD always encouraged Richard and believed in him when others did not. She never gave up on finding a way for Richard. Her encouragement served as a source of strength for me. I'm thankful that she crossed our path.

"Seraphina will treasure this beautiful card! It is a thoughtful gift for her 25th birthday." Richard has a friend who recently turned 25. Her name is Seraphina Kelsi Gravely. We saw an updated picture of Seraphina on Facebook a few weeks ago. She wore a vibrant silk royal blue gown, sapphire rings, Kendra Scott earrings, and a drop diamond necklace. She looked stunning! I think Richard has a crush on her, based on the broad smile and twinkle in his eyes when he sees her pictures.

Richard loves Seraphina's blue dress. That inspired him to get her a blue birthday card! Richard picked out this card for her when he went to the store the other day. The inside reads, "Treat yourself to everything! Happy birthday." It was sweet of him to pick this out for Seraphina!

"That looks outstanding! I will mail it tomorrow morning." I placed the card inside its blue envelope. Richard smiled as his computer monitor flashed on. He must have moved the mouse.

Richard Rhodes's point of view

CHAPTER EIGHT

As I gazed upon my computer monitors, I thought about Cameron. I'm glad that he liked my desk setup. He seemed like such an extraordinary person. I would have loved to become his friend. Unlike me, he probably has his own home. I bet his desk setup is excellent. I'm happy to know someone else was interested in the same things. Cameron made me feel included and not left out.

I sensed that Cameron treated everyone with the same enthusiasm and respect. When he spoke to me, it was as if my cerebral palsy didn't exist. It made me feel "normal." Cameron didn't ask me any questions about my wheelchair or communication board. Instead, we discussed something we both enjoyed. We were just regular guys talking about technology. Cameron would be one of my friends if I had a group of friends.

I've struggled to make friends for as long as I can remember. I've had limited opportunities to make friends because nobody approached me. I think they were afraid to, knowing it would be harder to converse with me.

I sometimes wish Mom had allowed me to attend public school. I know we made that decision together, but I did not understand how meaningful it was to build friendships. However, I understand Mom's reasoning for homeschooling me. She said she wanted me to get the best education that wasn't offered in our local schools. Mom also didn't want going to school to be traumatic for me. Parents can sometimes hold on too tight and not allow their kids to grow up.

I am thinking about creating my own Facebook account to broaden my circle. Mom is logged into her account on my computer, allowing me to see what everyone is doing. Occasionally, Mom posts a picture of me. When this happens, many people leave friendly comments. Some even ask how I am doing. I want to respond to them from my own account. Maybe I should ask Kekoa to help me set up my own Facebook account. Initially, I will only add a few people: my immediate family, aunts, and Kekoa.

Mom took my box of lights from the bag. "Do you want me to put your lights on your computer?" I was eager to see how they would look! I nodded. "Okay. It's great that they come with instructions!" I'm glad Mom's figuring out how to set them up. It's simple! The lights have adhesive strips on their backs. They stick to the back of the monitor and glow with a soft light powered by a USB port.

Mom opened the box and retrieved the lights. "Do you want these to go on the back of your right monitor?" I nodded. Mom plugged them into the USB port and centered them along the monitor's perimeter. She peeled back the adhesive strips and worked until all the lights adhered to the back edge of the monitor. I smiled broadly at her. The light's blue glow highlighted her face!

Watching Mom do anything that entails working on computers is funny. She needs help when she has to do anything that doesn't involve word processing or basic software. Mom utilizes computers for her job. They are just a tool for her. For me, they are my connection to the world.

My ability to work and understand computing is a part of who I am. I've watched hundreds of videos about computers and the latest technology. I could assist you with your computer difficulties if I didn't have limited mobility. If your computer experienced issues, I could inspect the monitor and check the connection of the HDMI cable. Sometimes, a computer malfunctions because of a simple cable error.

One day, Mom was having computer trouble. Her monitor was not coming on. I knew how to resolve the issue, so I attempted to instruct her on what to do. Mom didn't understand me, so she called a technician to help. The technician did what I tried to instruct her to do. At least her computer ended up getting fixed.

I know I don't have the dexterity to manipulate everything. However, I only need a willing pair of hands, and I can tell someone how to do something. Of course, it may take a little longer because I have to spell things out, but I am getting better at that. I discovered that working on computers is almost intuitive for me. People don't often understand that I know what I'm doing with computers. They only look at my physical limitations. They don't understand that the brain is the master of all your existence!

Mom installed the second set of lights on my left monitor. "They look awesome!" Mom's right! They do look awesome! "Can you believe I was able to put them on your monitors? Well, I guess this gives me some new career options." I found that so funny that I laughed for almost fifteen seconds! When I laugh this hard, it can cause my body to have more spastic movements. I popped myself in the eye when I tried to wipe away a laughter tear. Mom looked concerned, but she knew I do this often.

"I'm going to put your new shirt in the laundry. That way, it will be soft and clean when you wear it." Mom tossed the shirt a few feet. Surprisingly, it landed in the bathroom hamper!

I grasped the computer mouse's joystick, placed my thumb on the top, and moved the cursor across the screen. I love how Mom bought an adaptive computer mouse. That changed a lot for me. Now, I'm finally able to click on my own! I couldn't achieve that with a traditional mouse that requires index finger clicks.

Before finding the adaptive computer mouse, Mom was able to find an adaptive keyboard. The keyboard is larger than a traditional keyboard. It features large keys with bold letters and symbols. When I type, I can only manage one or two taps at a time. It is very time-consuming.

I located the Google Chrome icon. Conveniently, all the applications are located in the same place on my desktop, making them easy to find. My thumb trembled as I worked to press the button on my mouse. That can be frustrating. Most people don't have to work nearly as hard to do such a simple task. Google Chrome opened instantly. I'm impressed with how fast our internet is. Mom mentioned that we are on one of the best internet plans. That makes sense since she works from home, and I spend time on the computer. No wonder why we need a reliable internet connection!

I moved my arm and prayed it wouldn't jerk. I wanted to click on the search bar. Fortunately, I clicked it without any trouble. Next, I glanced at my keyboard and hovered my hand over several letters. I pressed my right knuckle on the Y. These splints help keep my hands in check so I can type. I always wear them when I get on the computer. If I didn't, it would be a disaster. The disaster would be an explosion of typos!

"Are you searching for YouTube?" I hummed. Before Mom realized what she did, she hummed back. I laughed hysterically! I knew Mom was not making fun of me. She just wasn't thinking! Mom laughed at herself and blushed. "Well, I hope you approve of my response, Mr. Rhodes. Did I do it right?" I shook my head as I laughed. I could tell that she was embarrassed. "Oh well! I can't be good at everything."

Mom makes me laugh a lot. She is a ton of fun, and my aunts thoroughly enjoy her company! I often wonder why she does not have a remarkable man in her life. I know my dad was not the right person for her. Some guy is missing out on having a relationship with a beautiful, loving, and intelligent woman. I wonder if Mom does not have a relationship because of me. I hope she knows I would be okay with it. I trust that she would not settle for anyone but the perfect man that God has prepared for her.

"What are you going to watch?" I kept my arm steady and clicked on the suggested search for YouTube. I had to wait and see what videos popped up. As soon as YouTube loaded, a video about the latest iPhone appeared in the recommended section.

I recall a time when phones had diverse styles. When I was young, Mom and I visited a store to find her a new phone. I was fascinated by the variety of phones available, particularly the ones that could slide and flip. Technology has always brought me endless joy.

A video about a drone caught my eye.
I always wanted a drone, but I can't operate one.
I wish I could fly one in the city or above cars.
Since I can't control a drone, I will watch
someone else fly it. I hovered over the video and
selected it with my adaptive mouse.

I noticed my desk was getting dusty. Once a
week, I ask one of my personal assistants to
clean my desk space. My keyboard and monitor
quickly accumulate dust. It's incredible how fast it
happens. My personal assistant takes everything
off my desk before wiping it down. After that, they
clean my keyboard and monitors. Mom says
I keep them busy. I see her point, but I do not
want my personal assistants to be bored to tears,
so I give them something to do.

I refer to my help as "personal assistants" or
"life auxiliaries." How fancy does that sound?
I don't use the word "sitter" because I am not a
baby. I think the word "sitter" sounds cringy.
I once heard someone refer to my assistants as
sitters. Someone at church asked Mom, "So how
many different sitters do you have working with
Richard now?" I don't think they meant anything
derogatory.

People do not fully understand the
relationship and the professionalism that is

required to support me. Mom took the opportunity to educate her gently. Mom said, "Richard has personal assistants or caregivers who help him perform daily tasks to enhance his quality of life. That way, he can be fulfilled as much as possible." You go, Mom! That is a great way to advocate!

In the video, a guy flew his drone with a remote controller. That reminded me of when I was smaller, and Mom bought me a remote-controlled car. She figured out a way for me to operate the remote control. Mom built up the controller's joystick knobs. That allowed me to grasp the knob between my index and middle fingers.

Mom would place the controller on my wheelchair tray. Then, I would put my fingers around the right joystick knob to move the car forward. Despite crashing the car into the wall endless times, I had so much fun. Mom didn't care because she knew I was happy. She was always glad to buy toys that I could play with.

This guy talked about how he spent over $1,000 on this drone! If I had a drone, I would use it to reach inaccessible places. Then, he flew it over buildings and trees. The view was unimaginable!

As the video continued, I drifted off into thought. This YouTube video reminded me of my dreams. You know how people say, "Only in your dreams." Well, my dreams are extraordinary! I've had dreams where I did not have any physical challenges. My abilities were very different!

In my dreams, I talk to all kinds of people. I also look like myself, except for a few changes. I am still tall and skinny but have more muscle in my arms and legs. My limbs do not look atrophied and thin. I do not have a blue wheelchair, a communication board, or a stiff body.

I even had a dream where I worked as an information technology technician! I absolutely loved that dream! I also had other dreams, such as driving a blue car and having a girlfriend. I decided not to tell Mom about those dreams. I'm scared of what she might think. Maybe it would break her heart.

One night, I dreamed about taking a beautiful woman to an elegant restaurant. I believe it is hard for Mom to think of me as a grown man. She tries to give me space and independence, but I don't think she can picture me as a husband or a dad. Many people do not realize that people with cerebral palsy can have the same things in life that anyone else has. However, cerebral palsy can affect the number of social experiences you encounter. I don't go many places without Mom. It can be hard to develop a relationship when your mom drives you around.

I also have serious dreams. There are dreams where I can talk to Mom with no trouble. I get to tell her how much I love and appreciate her. I can respond to her enthusiastically and not just hum and point to silent words on a laminated communication board. When I do that, I worry that it is boring to be around me. I don't want to be boring by slowly spelling out my words.

Some people think I am quiet. That is not true. I wish I could be more fluent with my speech and conversations. In my dreams, I talk to plenty of people and have plenty of friends. During one of my dreams, several guys and I started an IT business. If you were wondering, "Rhodes and Waller" is the name of our business!

In my dreams, I experience a completely different world. I am always thankful when I can have an extraordinary dream! I wonder if Mom also has remarkable dreams. I hope so because they are an incredible experience! It's like going on an adventure while you are asleep! Free entertainment if you ask me!

Then, the guy caught my attention. He explained that his brother got him into drones. It would be amazing to have matching drones with a sibling. There are times when I wish I had a brother or sister. I wouldn't care if they were older or younger than me. Having a brother would be fantastic! Mom told me they might pick on me for fun. She explained that is what siblings do to each other. I wouldn't care because I would love to have someone else around. Maybe my sibling would want to spend time with me.

If I had a younger brother, he might think I'm boring because I like computers. He also could take me for drives once he was old enough. My younger brother would probably participate in sports. Or maybe he would be a miniature version of me and enjoy working with computers too! That would be wonderful! If I had an older brother, maybe he could help care for me. I would look up to him and miss him after he moved out. My aunt's kids rarely come home. If it were me, I would often come home to visit Mom.

Mom likely never had another child because she knew I would need a lot of assistance. Let's be honest. I take up a lot of her time. My need for help is not bad because we all need help. However, I will think realistically about the matter.

I've learned that we all need people who bring out the best in us and hold us accountable. Kekoa, who is 19 years old, has been my personal assistant for the past year. She is the only person who is like a sibling to me. We are very close. Did I mention that she is beyond funny?

Kekoa is my best friend. When she is working with me, we just hang out. I often ask Mom to order food, and Kekoa grabs it once it's delivered. Sometimes, we even eat at my computer desk! I'm smart when it comes to reading people. I can tell if someone cares about me or if they are being friendly for a job. Kekoa is different. She does more than the basic things. She doesn't just try to find out what I want. She asks about me and how I am doing. If I'm feeling down, she will always ask why. Kekoa listens to me as opposed to me listening to her. She always gives me advice and shares what she would do.

Kekoa does more than any of my other personal assistants. She puts in extra effort and tries to build a relationship with me. For example, she takes me for drives to get me out of the house. Kekoa will drive me to get ice cream, and then we will eat it in the van! Sometimes, we even stroll around the mall for a change of scenery. Mom admires her a lot. I'm thankful Kekoa was recommended to us. I hope she never leaves because she is a blessing!

"I will be back in a few minutes. Does that sound good to you?" I grinned with approval. Mom kissed my head and walked out of my room. I always loved it when I had time to myself.

I want to experience being left alone for an extended period, but I never had that opportunity. Mom is never away for more than about thirty minutes. When she does leave me alone, she is always just somewhere in the house. Mom always makes sure that I will be okay before she leaves. I let her know that I would be fine. I want her to have more confidence in me. If I am sitting in my wheelchair, I will be okay for longer than thirty minutes. I don't need to be repositioned if I'm sitting up. I would be fine for hours if I had the TV on.

I'm not able to do everything by myself, but I still can be left alone. I know Mom doesn't want me to go without. However, she doesn't realize that I want to be recognized as someone who is capable. Maybe not physically, but I am mentally and emotionally capable of undertaking more adult responsibilities. It wouldn't be so bad to have an hour to myself. Park me in front of the

TV, and I will be okay! If you are concerned that I might need to use the bathroom, take me before you leave. I will not fall apart in an hour.

Don't get me wrong. I am thankful for everyone who helps care for me. Mom informed me that many families struggle to keep help. However, I want to spend more time alone. Just turn on the shower, step out, and let the warm water run over me for ten minutes. I would love to experience taking a relaxing shower by myself.

There are things I can do on my own. I'm not in denial that I need a load of assistance. However, I know what I can do. I am not entirely disabled, as people would say.

I respectfully do not prefer to use the word "disability." Let's take apart the word. The "dis" by definition means to "speak disrespectfully to or criticize." I am not being picky when I say this. I can't make this up! Look it up for yourself! When you put "dis" and "ability" together, it means to speak disrespectfully to or criticize ability!

I don't want my abilities criticized. We all have different abilities. Some people are great at art, while the next person may not have any art talent. We are all unique! It would be boring if everyone were made the same! Everyone has various abilities and talents! So, I like to say "varied ability" instead.

If someone were to use the word "disability" towards me, I would not be upset. I know it is a word used for situations like mine. Some people may be okay with using that word. It's all about personal preference. I choose to use "varied ability" instead.

"Are you doing okay, Richard?" Mom asked as she poked her head into my room. I nodded. "Alright. I am going to put the clothes in the dryer." I hope Mom knows how much I love her. She is beyond good to me. Mom has gone above and beyond for me for over two decades. I love her more than anyone knows.

Since Mom always puts me before herself, I wonder if that's why she doesn't have a boyfriend. I don't want to hold her back from living her life. Any guy should be proud to call her their own.

I wish I could express my appreciation to Mom by doing something special for her. I would love to buy her a large bouquet of roses or take her to a nice dinner. Unfortunately, I can only express my feelings by hugging her, attempting to kiss her, and using my communication board to tell her, "I love you" or "Thank you."

Speaking of talking to Mom, we have the same conversations over and over again. For example, she asks me things like:

"Do you need to go to the bathroom?"

"Are you hungry?"

"Are you thirsty?"

"Are you cold?"

"Is something wrong?"

"Do you feel bad?"

"Does your head hurt?"

"Does your back hurt?"

"Do your hips hurt?"

"Do you want to go to bed?"

"Do you want to turn to your side?"

"Do you want to take a shower?"

"Do you want to get on the computer?"

The list goes on and on. Mom does this when she is trying to figure out what I need. I know it is an effort for her or anyone else. Occasionally, they have to work hard to find out what I want.

Sometimes, Mom struggles to figure out what I need. I cannot access my communication board when I'm in bed. That makes things more challenging. To avoid some frustration, I pretend it's a game when Mom guesses wrong. I know that is silly, but it is how I cope. I call the game "10 questions" because Mom has to dig before stumbling on the right thing. When Mom guesses wrong, she gets a strike! Sometimes, she gets five strikes before coming close to finding out what I want. Most of the time, Mom gets it right on the second or third try. That takes a lot of skill. However, Mom's known me for 23 years. She's had tons of practice.

In the video, the drone flew over a massive field. The guy explained that this was close to where his cousin Kay lived. That name instantly reminded me of somebody from the clinic I attended.

In the clinic waiting room, a young woman named Kay also used a wheelchair. Kay was about 19 at the time. She had fake flowers woven through the spokes of her wheelchair. One day, Mom told her that she liked her "rolling throne." That made Kay's day. She smiled so big that it made the room glow!

One time, Kay wheeled past me, and I waved. Then Mom gave me a look and whispered, "Oh! She is beautiful." I wasn't going to let her know I thought Kay was pretty. However, there was this one girl who stood out the most. Her name is Mavie, and she was 18 at the time. Mavie always spoke to me in the waiting room. She was there because she took her brother to speech therapy.

Mavie wore a lot of black, and it always looked good on her. She admitted she wore black because it was classy. Mavie is gorgeous and was always fun to talk to. While I waited for my speech therapy session, she would sit beside me. One day, Mavie informed me that she overcomes Asperger's syndrome daily. I had no idea what that was, so I tapped the "?" on my communication board. She explained that Asperger's syndrome is a form of autism. I learned something new!

I never would have guessed she had that. Mavie has what people call an "invisible disability." That means she has challenges that are not visible. In contrast, my wheelchair is a giant visual hint. It is like an electronic billboard with a flashing sign that reads, "I need help."

I thought it was cool that Mavie could keep her "challenges" hidden. Later on, I regretted thinking that. One day, she told me about a time when teachers didn't believe that she had Asperger's syndrome. They told her that she was "normal." Mavie faced many challenges in school, but she overcame them all! That is truly remarkable!

I always enjoyed talking to Mavie. She made the clinic waiting room fun! She kept me entertained while I waited for my speech therapist. Mom would whisper, "Here comes your clinic girlfriend." I think she knew I had a secret crush on Mavie. I did because she was gorgeous and accepted me for who I am.

Mavie showed me pictures on her phone and let me look over her shoulder when she was on Instagram! It was enjoyable to engage in activities that people my age were also doing. One time, she even took a selfie with me. I should have asked her to text that picture to Mom, but I was too shy to ask.

One day, Mavie's little brother graduated from therapy. That means he no longer needs speech therapy. I found that out the hard way. I noticed that Mavie and her little brother stopped coming to the clinic. Luckily, her brother and I had the same speech therapist, Mary Grace.

I asked Mary Grace where Mavie went. She informed me that her brother graduated from speech therapy. At that moment, my heart sank because I lost my friend. That was a hard loss. I wished I asked her to text Mom that picture. That way, we would have her phone number. Mavie never knew that I looked forward to therapy every Tuesday and Thursday. It meant I got to talk to her.

That situation put me in a horrible mood. I told Mary Grace that I wasn't feeling good. She asked if I was sick. I nodded. I wasn't physically sick, but my heart felt sick. Mary Grace told me that she would let my mom know. A few minutes later, Mom came to get me. She let me leave therapy early because I worked hard for Mary Grace during all the previous sessions. On the ride home, I felt miserable.

There are times when I am in a bad mood or not feeling well. Mom always supports me during these times. Hearing her voice and knowing she's there is usually enough. Most of the time, she can console me. However, she couldn't that day. I was unhappy for the rest of that day.

I never told Mom what was wrong, but she eventually figured it out. While waiting at the clinic, Mom took my hand and said, "I miss her too. I tried looking her up on Facebook. She does not have an account." I knew Mavie didn't have Facebook. She has Instagram. Mom didn't have Instagram, so it was no use. It took me a while to get used to the dull waiting room. However, there were hilarious moments when Marcus entertained the waiting room!

I had speech therapy after a guy named Marcus Armani Langley. Like me, Marcus is nonverbal, uses a wheelchair, and has cerebral palsy. His older sister, Utopia, would bring him to therapy. Marcus wore hoodies and gold chains. He also loved to pick on the therapists! Marcus kept the clinic laughing! He would wheel into the clinic blasting rap music from his iPad! Utopia would get very embarrassed! She would tell him to turn his music down. Unlike me, Marcus can say a few simple words. "No" is his favorite word. I found it hilarious when Marcus gave his sister a hard time!

Mom entered the room and caught my attention. I smiled. Then, the guy from the video shared how he would travel to Italy. He informed his viewers that he would capture more drone footage there. After that, the video ended. Several suggested videos popped up, and I selected the first choice.

My right hand started to cramp, and I felt tired from using the computer mouse. I despise when my body wants to take a break when I want to keep going. My body is so disobedient sometimes! I am not giving up because I have time to rest later.

The next video started to play. In this video, the same YouTuber flew his drone over restaurants, nearby buildings, and a mall. The tops of the buildings looked like small squares until he flew close to them. It is a skill that he never crashed his drone into anything.

Next, the guy flew his drone close to the mall. When I go to the mall, I receive an abundance of stares. I call that place the "stare zone." I wish I could respond to people when they stare at me. Communication is such a struggle for me.

I don't understand why people feel sorry for me. Just because I get around differently doesn't mean I have a terrible life. I can think of situations worse than mine. People think I don't have any independence. That is not true! The people in jail do not have any independence!

There was a time when another guy using a wheelchair glanced at me. I could tell he felt sorry for me. Maybe it was because of my tray and communication board. That catches a lot of people's eyes. My tray is normal to me because I'm used to it. I see it as a desk. It's incredible how it attaches to my wheelchair! I have a desk and a chair combined into one! So, if you think about it, I have a portable office desk!

That reminds me of when Mom and I went to the mall. A kid pointed at me and said, "Look! He is stuck in a wheelchair!" Many people refer to individuals who use wheelchairs as "they are in a wheelchair." I get it. Yes, we are physically sitting in the wheelchair. However, we don't sit in them forever! It's not like we sleep in them at night, even though I fall asleep in mine sometimes!

Wheelchair users transfer out of their wheelchairs. We are not stuck in our equipment! I use the phrase "using a wheelchair" instead of "in a wheelchair." A wheelchair is a tool that transports individuals from one point to another. It's constructed with metal and tires, similar to a vehicle! Some people act like a wheelchair is a prison and that it is "confining." In reality, it gives people freedom! It makes getting around possible for me! So, how is that a bad thing?

Thinking about this made me remember when a young boy came to me and asked, "Do you ride that all the time?" They were referring to my wheelchair. I burst into laughter and gave a nod. He smiled back before walking off. I thought what he asked was hilarious! He saw my wheelchair as a ride instead of something confining. I wish everyone felt the same way.

There was, however, another time when someone else was not as friendly. I was rolling through the mall when a teenage guy stared at me. I heard him say, "What the heck is wrong with him!" Mom noticed the smile disappear from my face. She leaned down and whispered, "There's an "A" in every crowd!" That instantly put me in a good mood! I laughed so hard that my feet kicked out! Mom always knew how to make me feel better!

The video's scene switched, and the transition was amazing! This guy flew his drone in many different locations! He was showing footage from when he flew it over the snow slopes in Colorado.

The snow reminded me of ice skating. Last December, Mom and I went ice skating! I never thought it would be possible for me to ice skate. However, Mom told me it was possible! She is so good at problem-solving! Mom pushed me on the ice rink, and I had the time of my life! It felt like I was flying! I wondered if that's what it felt like to run. Surprisingly, it wasn't as cold as I thought it would be. Mom wrapped a blanket around me, and I was all set!

After we went ice skating, I realized something! If Mom can push me on an ice rink, she can also push me on a rollerblade rink! It would be cool to go and look at all the overhead lights! I asked Mom if she would take me rollerblading. She said we would go when it isn't busy. Maybe I should ask if Keoka can come! That would be exciting!

That reminds me of another memory from forever ago. When I was 14, I told Mom that I wanted to ride a roller coaster. I wonder how she handles all these situations with such grace. Mom had a great solution! She explained that it is like sitting in a chair that goes remarkably fast! So, Mom pushed me all around the house! She was running and quickly turning the corners in our hallway. Mom told me not to be afraid because she had an iron grip on my wheelchair. I wasn't scared because I was having a blast! I'm thankful that she gave me that experience!

I peered over at Mom. She sat in the chair next to my bed and scrolled on her phone. When I laughed aloud, she looked up at me and smiled. I wish everyone had such a loving person in their life. I think about how she will not always be able to help me. There will be a day when she will die. I'm not worried so much about her dying. I know she will transition to her place in heaven, but what will happen to me? Will there be other loving and caring people who understand what a miracle my life is? Will I have a wife who feels like a wife rather than a glorified assistant?

We are all vessels of clay. We think if a pot breaks, then it cannot be used. The truth is that it can be repaired and become better than before. My vessel is broken. However, I have been "fixed" through the miracle of God's redemption plan. I know my physical healing is on its way. In the meantime, I will do what I can until I attain my healing in heaven. Spiritually, I have been cleaned and glued together perfectly, just like when you mend a clay pot. I can now serve my intended purpose, regardless of how that looks.

I looked at the monitor. The drones flew over mountains! I enjoyed the view of the freezing mountains from my warm room. Then, the drone guy wrapped up the video. He said he plans to film more content and asked us to subscribe.

I was tired of being on the computer for now. My hands also hurt from my splints. The splints keep my usually bent wrists straight. So, my wrists felt stretched. I hummed to get Mom's attention. She peered up from her phone. I touched my left splint with my right hand. "Are you ready to take those off?" I nodded. Mom removed my left hand from the splint and did the same for my right hand. That felt sufficiently better!

CHAPTER NINE

"It's getting late. Are you hungry?" Mom asked. I shook my head. I didn't feel like eating tonight. When I eat noodles, they fill me up for the rest of the day. Since I've been home, I haven't burned many calories. On the days that I exercise, I tend to eat a lot more.

Today, I also barely needed to use the bathroom. It's not always like that. It's only that way today because I didn't drink much. My Aunt Julie thinks I need to drink more water. She's right. I need to do better.

"Let me know if you get hungry. I think I'll have my leftovers from lunch. Do you want to come to the kitchen with me, or do you have plans to do something else?" I looked at my bedroom door. Mom put my splints away and pushed me into the hallway.

Our hallway is massive, and Mom has it decorated beautifully! It has an enormous window on the left side and artwork on the right. I am not trying to brag, but Mom has our house looking like it came out of a magazine!

As we entered the kitchen, Mom's phone rang. "They will have to wait." Mom is good about that. She always tries to make our time together about our interactions. At restaurants, I see parents glued to their phones and ignoring their children. I'm thankful that Mom is all about our relationship.

I wheeled next to the table as Mom retrieved her leftover rice. I felt terrible because she didn't eat much earlier. She was too busy feeding me.

When it comes to eating, I'm used to being fed. However, there are certain things I can eat on my own. I can eat large food items like baked pretzels or chicken strips. However, I can't dip chicken strips in their sauce because I will make a mess. If I want anything like popcorn or chips, I have to have help. My favorite food is various styles of yakisoba noodles. I will always need help eating those. Sometimes, I spill them on my shirt and get to wear them! That's not exactly what I want, but it happens! The good news is that Mom keeps an extra shirt packed in the van just in case.

Mom always wants me to look nice. Maybe it is so people can focus on my outfit instead of my wheelchair. There are limited clothing options that work well for me. Mom will never admit it, but dressing me must be difficult. Due to my spastic movements, I usually wear clothing that is a size larger and made of stretchy fabrics. Unfortunately, there are a limited amount of stretchy dress clothes for men. I have many Polo shirts that are one size too big, and the same goes for my pants. My pants are a little loose around the waist, which makes it easier for Mom to pull them on and off me. When I sit down, you can't tell they are bigger, so everything works out.

I was startled when the microwave beeped. Mom sat beside me, took my hand, and bowed her head. I closed my eyes. "Thank You, God, for this food. Thank You for a wonderful day. Thank You for abundantly blessing us. We know all good comes from You. We thank You, God, for Your constant love. Amen." Mom gently squeezed my hand. I always thought it was precious when Mom prayed. Years ago, she told me that prayers are the best gift you can give someone. What Mom doesn't know is that I pray for her in my head. I pray for her strength and happiness.

Mom and I sat in silence as she started to eat her rice. I love the silence between people who care for each other. A lot of people are afraid of silence. They always think there needs to be some chatter going on. However, Mom and I are okay with it because we enjoy each other's company.

"Let's see who called. Aunt Lindsay! Let's call her back," Mom said as she called my aunt. The phone rang and rang before Aunt Lindsay finally picked up. "Hey! I'm eating right now. Richard is here with me. Do you want to talk to him?" I heard laughter from the other end. "It's switching to FaceTime." Mom tapped her phone's screen. FaceTime is how I communicate with people during phone calls. It allows them to see my body language.

Our FaceTime instantly connected. You can thank our fast internet for that! Mom held her phone up so I could see my aunt. "Oh my gosh! Hello Richard," Aunt Lindsay greeted as she waved at me. I attempted to wave back. "How was your day?" I smiled in return.

I wanted to tell her about my day, but my arms felt stiff. Reaching the words at the bottom of my communication board is a challenge.

I decided it wasn't worth it and sat still. Unfortunately, I had to do this a lot. It is difficult to coordinate my body enough to touch a single word.

There are days when my muscles are extra tight, or my energy level is low. On those days, I only communicate what is necessary. I don't have the luxury to comment on everything. However, I don't want to live inside my head. I have to keep reminding myself that just because it is easier does not mean it is what's best for me. I want to optimize every ability that I have.

Here is something I wish everyone knew. The fact that I am a person comes before my diagnosis. Please don't confuse my silence with apathy or a lack of intelligence. I have thoughts just like everyone else. When people talk to me, I always answer them in my head. Even if all you get is a nod or a hum, I answered you. My thoughts are more in-depth than the reply I give on my communication board. Those replies are simple and get the basic thought across. When Mom asks how my day is, I tell her about it in my head. When a personal assistant asks me what I think about something, I give them a detailed answer in my head. When I watch a video, I have opinions floating in my brain.

"We decided what to get for your birthday! It is something massive and fancy! You are going to love it." I wondered what it was.

I hummed with excitement! I'm thankful I don't have to feel nervous around my aunts. They understand me and don't judge me. Some people may think I am strange. I am comfortable being myself, while others may feel afraid or uncomfortable. For example, I may hum loudly to get Mom's attention. When I do, people turn their heads and stare as if I did something wrong. We all make sounds when we talk. What makes my humming any different? It's my way of conversing.

I know that my communication style differs from how others express themselves. Over the years, I've learned that those who really care about me will work with me to understand me.

"It's going to be something you can use every day!" "Lindsay, that's enough hints for now! If you keep that up, he will figure out what it is." Mom shut her down! I found it amusing when Mom and her friends talked to each other!

"Are you trying to guess what it is?" Aunt Lindsay asked. "That's for me to know and for you to find out," I replied in my head and grinned. That phrase is one of my favorite things to think to myself. I know a great deal, but there is plenty everyone else has to find out.

"What are you eating, Jamie? What did you cook tonight?" "We went out to lunch today. You can only guess where he picked! So, I am having rice." Rice is good, but Mom's cooking is always the best. Sometimes, I sit in the kitchen and watch her cook. Mom claims I help her by being her observer and taste tester!

"Where is your plate, Richard?" "He took a nap and got on his computer for a while. After that, he said he still wasn't hungry." Mom mentioning my nap reminded me of when I was younger. Growing up, I was never able to get in trouble. The most trouble I would ever get in was Mom saying, "Look at me." Sometimes, she would gently turn my head to look me in the eyes. At the very worst, she would say, "Richard Metoyer Rhodes" with a serious tone. Mom never grounded me because I never needed to be. Maybe it was also because she didn't have much to ground me from.

When I was younger, the only mischievous thing I remember doing was pretending to be asleep. I did that so I could eavesdrop! My personal assistant would be with me, and Mom would sometimes come and visit with them.

Maybe Mom didn't want them to be bored. When I was "asleep," Mom talked to them about various things. I would keep my eyes shut and try not to laugh. When I pretended to be asleep, I heard Mom talk about herself or my aunts. She would even discuss my aunt's husbands and what they planned to get their wives for Christmas! Mom refers to my aunt's husbands as my "uncles." They are all very friendly.

I was spying, but it was the only bad thing I could do. Eventually, my luck ran out. One day, Mom and my personal assistant were talking, and I laughed! Mom didn't get mad at me. All she said was, "Well, it sounds like Richard has been awake!" After that, she kissed my forehead.

There was another time when something else hilarious happened. While Mom was talking with my personal assistant, she sat in my wheelchair! I was in bed watching a movie when my personal assistant needed advice from Mom. I guess Mom thought the conversation would last a while. There isn't another chair in my room except for the one beside my bed. So, Mom got my wheelchair and parked it beside my personal assistant. I found it hilarious, but it made sense! Mom needed to sit down, so she found the closest chair available!

"What did you do on the computer today?" It's times like this when I want to say something in detail. I'd love to tell her about the incredible drone footage. However, it would take a very long time to spell out. It would take minutes upon minutes. When I'm slowly spelling out my responses, I occasionally lose my train of thought on what I want to say. This happens because I'm too focused on spelling out the first part. That makes it difficult for me to keep up in conversations.

Sometimes, I let Mom talk on my behalf. I let her answer for me if the reply would take me ten minutes to spell. "He watched drone footage. This man was flying his expensive drone. He flies his drone anywhere he visits. Richard enjoyed watching it." For the most part, Mom covered what I wanted to say. I would have added that I'd also love to fly a drone. "That sounds like something you would enjoy watching."

Mom placed her empty bowl into the dishwasher. "Richard, I am going to go and check on your uncle. I left him working in the garage! You know how he is with getting himself into all kinds of trouble. I love you. It was good talking to you," Aunt Lindsay said and blew a kiss to me. I pretended to catch the kiss. "Good luck, Lindsay! Talk to you later!" My aunt smiled and hung up.

Mom walked to the sink and retrieved my blue cup. I use a cup with a lid and straw to take my evening medicine. "Do you want ice in your water?" I shook my head.

"Do you want to go brush your teeth?" I love how Mom tries to give me choices that I have control over. She attempts to promote my independence as much as possible. I smiled. Mom placed my drink on my tray. I held onto my cup as we approached my room.

As Mom wheeled me into my room, I noticed the new lights behind the computer monitors. They looked outstanding in their new place!

Mom rolled me into the bathroom and took my baclofen from the pill bottle. I opened my mouth as she placed the pill inside. I take this medicine every night before bed. It helps my muscles to chill out and not be as tight. I used the straw to take a drink.

"Did Kekoa shave your face last night?" I nodded. "Okay. It doesn't look like you need your face shaved tonight." Mom applied water and toothpaste to my U-shaped electric toothbrush. She then handed it to me. I bit down on the U-shaped toothbrush and held the mouthpiece in place. Mom pressed the power button.

My gums tickled as I moved the mouthpiece around. This excellent toothbrush allows me to brush my teeth independently. Before Mom bought this U-shaped electric toothbrush, she had to brush my teeth. Who would have thought such a simple piece of equipment could make a difference in my life?

After I finished, I took a sip of water and placed my cup on the bathroom counter. Mom handed me a washcloth, and I wiped my face clean. "Do you need to use the bathroom?" I shook my head. I don't need to go right now, but I probably will need to in the middle of the night. That's what usually happens.

"The clothes in the dryer need to be folded. Do you want to stay here or come help me?" I looked in the direction of my bedroom door. Mom understood that I wanted to go with her. "Aww. That is sweet. Thank you. I will appreciate your help." Mom wrapped her arm around me. I smiled and leaned my head onto her. It is difficult to hug, especially with a wheelchair tray in front of me.

Folding clothes may seem like a menial task. However, intentionally including a person with exceptionalities in any activity has a significant impact on their self-esteem. God did not design humans to be takers. God created us to be givers. I want to give all I can, even if it is just a smile that can make someone's day.

Mom taught me how to be a selfless giver. My heart is full of love and gratitude for all she has done for me. Mom also helps other people in many different ways. I think that is how a person should be when they have all their priorities appropriately aligned. When someone has true joy, they cannot help but share it with others. Joy does not mean that you don't have any problems in life. Joy is a place of contentment regardless of the circumstances around you. I'm not there yet, but that is my goal. I try to have a vertical view of life while sitting on a horizontal surface.

Mom rolled me into the hallway. As we approached the kitchen, I noticed how clean the house was. Our house is always in order because she keeps it clean.

After we entered the laundry room, Mom opened the dryer. "Here are the towels." Mom draped one around my shoulders. It felt warm! Then she pulled the towels out of the dryer and plopped them on my tray. Mom says I help her with the laundry by keeping her company while she folds. I also assist by using my tray as a table for the clothes.

Mom folded a towel while the other warm towels covered my arms. It felt incredible! "I've had a wonderful time spending today with you. Did you have fun today?"

There are moments like this when I feel the urge to cry. There is so much I want to tell my mom, but I can't. I want to tell her how much I enjoyed spending today with her. I had to force these thoughts away. If I didn't, I would feel unhappy.

I attempted to grab a towel. After two attempts, I got my hand around its edge. Then, I raised my right arm and lifted the towel. "Thank you." Mom quickly folded it. "I'm going to need the one wrapped around you!" She lifted the towel from around my shoulders. Mom danced as she folded the final towel. She was so entertaining!

All of a sudden, my back started to itch. I raised my hand. "What is it?" I scratched my hand. When I do this, Mom knows I'm itching somewhere. "Is it your head?" I shook my head. "Is it your neck?" I shook my head again. "Is it your back?" I nodded. Sometimes, Mom would ask me if it was my upper or lower back. This time, she scratched my back all around. It felt wonderful!

"Did I get the spot?" I grinned. Mom continued to scratch my back. She always went above and beyond. Even if I didn't have an itch, it felt fantastic to have my back rubbed or scratched. That's something I cannot do whenever I feel like it. So, I always enjoy it when it happens.

"I bet you are tired of being in this boring laundry room." I shook my head and took Mom's hand. "It is beautiful outside tonight. The moon is lighting up the sky! Would you like to go sit outside?" I smiled broadly. I didn't care what we did. I just enjoyed spending time with her.

CHAPTER TEN

Mom's wine cabinet caught my eye as we passed through the kitchen. I've wanted to try alcohol. However, Mom won't let me try it. One evening, we were out to dinner with my aunts, and Aunt Ashley ordered a white wine. I pointed at her drink. Mom shook her head and whispered, "That would be dangerous for you. You cannot drink alcohol due to the medications that you take. Mixing alcohol and medications can be harmful." All I did was nod in return.

"I love you," Mom said with a gentle voice. "Mm-hmm," I replied and covered my face. "Mm-hmm" is my sassier response, meaning, "I know you love me." When I say, "Hmmm," it is a gentle and quiet hum. It is a sweet sound, which is my way of responding "I love you" to Mom's "I love you." I sometimes like to tease her and say, "Mm-hmm" instead. She understands and thinks it's funny!

"Alright, noodle head." Mom calls me by a nickname more than my actual name. She has many nicknames for me. They range from sweetheart, sweetie, handsome, noodle head, and Mr. Rhodes. When I was younger, Mom called me "curly cue" because of my curly hair. Since I've gotten older, she stopped calling me that. Thank God.

Mom opened the glass door that led to our back porch. She then gently pushed me outside. A cool breeze brushed my face, and it felt wonderful. Our back porch is fantastic. It has clear lights across the ceiling, creating a warm and inviting glow.

Mom turned on the outdoor ceiling fans and pulled a chair beside me. She preferred to be at my eye level as an act of respect. "The sky is full of stars tonight." I know Mom told me that because I couldn't see them. However, I could see the moon.

I felt Mom take my hand. My fingers naturally clenched tightly around hers. I know she loves me and would do anything for me. Mom's kindness reminded me of a time when I was having a rough night. It was because I had a difficult time communicating that day. Mom knew something wasn't right, but I could not tell her what was wrong. So, I asked if we could go for a drive. It was 9:45 at night and completely dark outside. Mom did not care. She loaded me in the van and drove me around for an hour. We went to a drive-through and bought cokes. Then we looked at the beautiful town. It felt wonderful to get out and diffuse. After we got back home, I felt so much better!

"This is very relaxing. I will invite your aunts over this week. We can eat dinner out here and enjoy this weather." I always loved it when my aunts came to visit. I wonder what day of the week Mom was thinking. Was it Monday night? Wednesday night? Who knows!

Since I can't quickly ask questions, I sometimes decide to wait things out. If I wonder about something, I wait and see for the answer. I've learned that I will be okay without knowing the answer. It won't hurt me not to find out! It annoys me, but my brain moves on to something else shortly after. In this situation, I will eventually know what day they will come. Mom will tell me at some point!

Then, my thoughts drifted away. I do this a lot because I keep to myself. I remember when

Mom hosted a family night at our house. She cooked dinner for my aunts and cousins. After we ate, Mom thought everyone should tell a funny story. Each person told a funny story about themselves. I remember feeling sad because I did not have a funny story prepared. There was no way that I could spell out a story word by word. When it became my turn, I just shook my head. I would have loved to share a funny story between Aunt Lindsay and me.

Here is how that story goes. I was waiting in the van with my Aunt Lindsay while Mom shopped in the store. I didn't want to go inside because Mom only needed a few things. Meanwhile, Aunt Lindsay watched for people to park in the accessible parking spaces beside us. She made me laugh because she said sarcastic things when people pulled into those parking spaces. I remember her saying, "You better have a blue VIP tag to hang in your window! If not, you can get towed away! All I have to do is call! Richard, don't let me get out of this van! I will set them straight!" I wished I could have shared that story with everyone. However, I knew Aunt Lindsay would remember the time we had together.

Mom let go of my hand and placed her arm around me. I tilted my head to the left in a hug-

like manner. I then looked down at my words and slid my hand over to the square that read, "Thank you." Mom smiled and asked, "For what?"
I looked down at my communication board and located the letter "E." Next, I placed my right index knuckle on the "E." Then, I searched for the "V." I found it and continued to do the same thing as I spelled E. V. E. R. Y. T. H. I. N. G. Mom is always very patient when I do this. She follows along with every letter that I choose before stringing them together. "You deserve it. I love you more than all the stars in the sky."

Even though I couldn't see the stars above me, I knew there were plenty! When I can't see something, I get on the computer and search for a picture! I've seen pictures of stars online. I know there are millions of stars above! Mom must love me more than a ton!

I know caring for me is hard work, both mentally and physically. There are days when I look at Mom's eyes and see how she aches for me because of the pain that I am in. There are mornings when she comes in to see me, and I notice the circles under her eyes. I can't help but think that she is a selfless individual. Mom is the generous person that God intended for her to be.

I turned my head and kissed Mom's cheek. She teared up. I saw the moonlight glisten off the tears in her eyes. I wish I could just say, "It is okay. I love you." Mom hugged me and then rubbed my shoulder. "You, Mr. Rhodes, are a good son. I love you more than all the radiant stars in the night sky."

As much as I wanted this precious moment to last, my feet started to hurt. I lifted my right leg for a second, but that didn't help. My shoulders were also in pain.

I raised my hand to get Mom's attention. "What is it?" I pointed to the picture of a bed on my communication board. "Do you want to go to your room?" I knew she would ask that. I smiled. Mom turned off the outdoor ceiling fans and rolled me inside.

We passed through our elegant hallway and turned into my room. "Is there anything you need to do before getting in bed?" I shook my head. Mom parked me next to the bed and locked my wheels. My bed was already lowered from when I got up earlier. "Are you ready?" Mom asked as she unbuckled my seat belt. I nodded. Mom leaned in and hugged me. I placed my right arm around her back. "I love you too. It's time for the final transfer of the day."

Mom tries to get me in bed before I become overly tired. When I'm exhausted, it's harder for me to assist with transfers.

I put my feet on the floor. Mom placed her arms around me, and I wrapped mine around her neck. "On Three. One. Two. Three." I stood to my feet and turned my head to the left. Then I stepped with my right foot toward the bed, followed by my left foot. Mom balanced me as I held onto her.

Mom helped me turn before I felt the edge of the bed behind my legs. "You are there." I sat down. Mom removed my house shoes and raised the head of the bed. She then placed her left arm behind my back and her right arm under my knees. In one swift motion, Mom rotated and laid me down. She is incredibly strong. Maybe this isn't hard for her since she's done it for 23 years. "Do you want the bed to be flat?" I nodded. Mom grabbed the remote and lowered the head of the bed.

"Do you want to watch a video?" I smiled. Mom turned on my giant flat-screen TV, which was mounted to the wall on the right side of my bed. Mom selected the YouTube app. "What do you want to watch?" I watched as she slowly selected each video option.

Mom selected several videos before a recommended video caught my attention. It was one of my favorite kinds of videos! I enjoy the "night drive point of view" videos. I love these videos because the driver records them from the driver's seat. It gives me the feeling of driving a car!

I let out a loud hum! "Okay!" Mom selected the video. "I am going to go get ready for bed." I grinned. Mom placed a kiss on my cheek and left the room.

I glanced at the TV and saw a guy back out of his driveway. If I could drive, I would go for joy rides when it was dark outside. Everything looks more remarkable at night! The buildings glow like neon lights!

I wish I could drive. When I was younger, I looked up the driver's manual to study for the written test. I seriously read every page of that driver's manual. I know I will never be able to drive. However, I knew I was capable of learning how. After I read the entire driver's manual, I took the online practice tests. I enjoyed taking them because they made me think through challenging scenarios! I took multiple practice tests until I achieved a perfect score. Mom couldn't believe it! She was incredibly proud and said I earned a driving lesson!

Mom rolled me into the van and gave me an hour-long driving lesson! I observed how she switched lanes, merged into traffic, and passed other vehicles. She showed me where the hazard lights were and explained what to do if there was ice on the road. Everything she explained made sense. I knew I was capable of learning the rules of the road!

After that, there were times when I told Mom that I wished I could drive. Mom explained that my van was my vehicle, and she was my chauffeur! Mom always knew how to make me feel better.

I grinned as I watched from the driver's seat. The video was taking me into town. One time, Mom walked in as I was watching one of these videos. She asked, "Where are you headed?" I burst into laughter!

Then, my thoughts shifted to when Mom had to go out of town for a business trip when I was 16. My Aunt Julie stayed with me that weekend. We had a lot of fun! My favorite part was when she helped me transfer to a driving arcade game! She would press the gas pedal while I would steer! Aunt Julie placed so many quarters in that machine! I remember her getting more quarters because I wanted to keep going!

I love my Aunt Julie. She is a licensed practical nurse who is compassionate and hilarious! When I was 14, I told her I wanted to be normal like her kids. I vividly remember Aunt Julie saying, "Richard, what is normal? Who wants to be normal? Where is the fun in that? God makes no mistakes. Please always remember that." She's right. Where would the fun be in the world if we were all made the same? She always has a way of making me feel better. I'm grateful to be surrounded by such uplifting people.

I heard a gentle knock on my door. "Hey!" Mom smiled as she took my hand. I wondered how she still carried a smile despite it being so late. She had to be exhausted by now.

"Is there anything you need before I go to bed?" I raised my hand and turned my head to the right. Mom placed her hands under my left shoulder and left hip. "Try to bring your left arm over and reach for the opposite side of you." Mom bent my knees.

Mom continues to help me practice bed mobility. She reassures me that it's okay if I can't do it. However, it is still good for me to assist.

Years ago, Mom attached a bed rail to the right side of my bed to help me turn onto my side. I tried to grab the rail many times, but my left arm couldn't stretch far enough to reach it. We even tried moving it to the left side of the bed, but that didn't work either. As a result, I need someone to help me turn onto my side.

I leaned and reached to the right as Mom gently pushed me under my left shoulder and hip. I'm unsure if I was of any help, but I gave it my all. In no time, I was on my side. It felt better to be off my back.

I appreciate how Mom makes sure that I am comfortable. Hopefully, I will sleep well tonight. If I'm lucky, I will only wake up once or twice.

Then, I heard a thumping sound. "Ow! That hurt!" "Are you okay?" I asked in my head. "Richard, I hit my leg on the bed frame. I'm glad I didn't break it!"

In the past, Mom and I joked that we had the perfect plan if she injured her leg. I would let her use my backup wheelchair! We always keep my previous manual wheelchair in case my current one needs repair. Right now, it is in the hallway closet.

I motioned toward the TV and shook my head. "What do you want to do now?" I closed my eyes and opened them. "You look tired. Do you want me to turn this off?" I nodded.

Mom turned off the TV and took my hand. "Thank You, Lord, for a great day with my son. Thank You for allowing Richard to feel well today. Most of all, thank You for all that You do for us. Amen." I squeezed Mom's hand and nodded in agreement.

Mom kissed my forehead and pulled up the covers. "Have a good night's sleep. Kekoa will be here soon. I love you." She turned off the light and partially closed the door as she exited down the hall. Now, I was alone again with my thoughts.

Before I fall asleep, I usually take some time to have a conversation with God. I know He knows every thought that is in my head. I do not have a language barrier with God. He understands me perfectly!

I'm thankful that Mom taught me how important it is to have God in my life. I thank Him for how He works in my life. Others may not understand and think I have nothing to be thankful for. However, I live my life with the perspective that it is a miracle.

I pondered my purpose in this world. Could my purpose be to instill strength in my mom and others? Or is it something entirely different? What if my purpose is unique for each individual in my life? The possibilities are endless!

What I do know is that I am proud of who I am! I'm pleased with what I have accomplished so far. However, I am not done! My story is far from over! I'm still young and have so much life left to live. My next big goal is to work for Mom's business. Just because things are more challenging for me doesn't mean they are impossible. The only difference is that I have a different way of getting things done. I am thankful for my challenges. Challenges let you know that you are alive! I would rather be neck-deep in fear than be bored and stagnant. To reach for the stars, you have to jump!

In God's eyes, we are all equal. Our abilities do not define our value as human beings. We all possess unique talents and gifts. Therefore, we all deserve to be treated with love and respect.

I am not a nobody. I am not a burden. I am a vessel of miracles! That means I hold many miracles. My life's story is a miracle because I overcame many obstacles! I have faced numerous challenges on many days of my life.

However, those challenges ended in victories! The best part about the darkness is that you can rise out of it! The best part about the valleys in life is that you don't always stay there. You have to climb out of those valleys day by day. Before you know it, you will be standing at the mountaintop! Once you arrive, the view is magnificent! It is a radiant sight that will shine in your heart forever!

On the other hand, this is not all about me. Everyone has a purpose in this world. We are all vessels. Vessels of miracles!

Seven years later

Richard Rhodes's point of view

EPILOGUE

Veronica is spectacular! She was trying to set up one of my new monitors. "So, I connect the cord to this. Okay. That makes sense."

My wife brings me tremendous joy! She is exceptional and always supportive. She loves me for who I am. Veronica also understands cerebral palsy a great deal. I know she's had plenty of experience because of her brother, Jared. He is similar to me, yet very different.

Jared is Veronica's older brother by two years. He has cerebral palsy, uses an electric wheelchair, and communicates with a Tobii Dynavox. His fancy communication device is mounted to his electric wheelchair. He types with his eyes better than I could when I tried that device many years ago.

Aside from that, Jared has long, chest-length black hair that is parted down the center. He wears all black with his circular gold antique glasses. The other week, he wore black jeans and an AC/DC T-shirt. His wife, Olympia, also wears a lot of black. Olympia is very kind and complements Jared perfectly.

"Oh man," Veronica murmured as she attempted to power the monitor. I knew how to fix it, but I couldn't do it immediately. I wheeled forward to get a clearer view of the project.

I tapped the words "off" and "on" on my communication board and pointed at the power button. "¿Por qué no pensé en eso, Ricardo?" I shook my head. I had no idea what Veronica said, but I knew she spoke Spanish when she got annoyed.

After graduating high school, Veronica moved to Mexico with her best friend, Emilee. She relocated to that area because Emilee's family lived there. Veronica lived in Mexico for five years and learned to speak Spanish!

Veronica pressed the power button and held it for a few seconds. A blue light glowed, and the monitor lit up. "Yes," I thought to myself. "Finally!" Veronica wrapped her arms around me. I wanted to hug her back, but I couldn't because of how I was sitting.

Veronica's care for me is a steady light in my life. Her compassionate heart shines, and she is always ready to offer support and kindness. With her ability to spread positivity, she uplifts those around her, creating a ripple effect that spreads hope and reassurance.

"I didn't think it would be that easy. It only took about five minutes to set up," Veronica said as she leaned against my wheelchair's tray and gazed into my eyes. I placed my hand on top of hers. I wanted this moment to last because it was how I could thank her. However, Veronica stood up and rearranged something on my desk. "Do you like the way this looks?" I nodded because I loved anything she did for me.

Then, I pointed to my communication board. Veronica placed her arm around me as I touched the word "off." "Do you want to turn the computer off?" I tapped my wheelchair's tray. Veronica removed the tray. I took her hand and placed my other hand on my lap.

Veronica sat in my lap and turned sideways. Her legs hung over my wheelchair's right armrest as she wrapped her arms around my neck. Now, I can see her up close! I can see her beautiful dark brown eyes and natural long brown curly hair.

I wrapped my arms around her skinny waist. "I love you, Richarda. Te quiero mucho, Richarda," Veronica stated. I kissed her cheek, and her smile rose like a sunrise.

I admire how Veronica sees me for who I am instead of my physical challenges. It is precious that we are celebrating our one-year wedding anniversary next month! That is a milestone that felt unimaginable just a few years ago. Veronica has changed my life in ways I never imagined. I once believed that love and marriage were out of reach for me. Now, we are building our future together.

Veronica and I have our own house. We live in the same neighborhood as my mom. Mom comes over several times a week for dinner. Veronica's parents, Melinda and Conner, live two hours away. We get to see them at least once a month. Even though Veronica and I are both 31 years old, we are still very close to our parents.

Jared is Veronica's only sibling. He and Olympia live thirteen hours away in Florida. They visit us during the holidays, and we always have a wonderful time with them!

Reflecting on my life, I often find myself in profound awe. Since I was young, I passionately clung to my dreams. Now, the reality I live in surpasses anything I ever imagined. I am thankful that God has attentively listened to my heartfelt prayers. My life is a vibrant testament to the incredible power of faith. Now, I have a devoted wife who lovingly stands by my side and an inviting home that resonates with my laughter and Veronica's joy. My journey showcases how unwavering faith in God can ignite extraordinary miracles!

If you were to inquire about my heart's greatest desire, you might assume it would revolve around the ability to walk or talk.

However, the truth is I feel immeasurably blessed just as I am. How could I wish for more when my life is so rich and fulfilling? I find peace and contentment in the blessings that surround me. My most sincere longing is to develop an even closer connection with my Lord and Savior. I am a vessel prepared for His use. Filled with His miracles, I am eager to share them to inspire and uplift those around me, including you!

ABOUT THE AUTHOR

I was born in Slatina, Romania, in 1998. I was left in an orphanage, but God had a plan for me! I was adopted when I was 19 months old. After that, I came to America!

My life took a significant turn when I was 12. That was the year I was diagnosed with Asperger's syndrome. It was a revelation that brought clarity to my family. A diagnosis is not the end of the world. It is the beginning of understanding!

My life has been a series of challenges, but I've never faced them alone. I've overcome every obstacle with God by my side and the unwavering support of those who believed in me.

When I was a senior in high school, I chose to become an occupational therapist assistant. My decision was fueled by my deep understanding of being different and my profound compassion for others. I knew their struggles because I had lived them. On December 16, 2021, I proudly graduated with my degree as an occupational therapy assistant.

I am deeply passionate about advocacy, raising awareness, and helping people. I believe God uses me as His vessel to minister and share His love with others.